IT HAPPENED
IN HANOI

It Happened in Hanoi

Vernon L. Anley

RESOURCE *Publications* · Eugene, Oregon

Resource Publications
A division of Wipf and Stock Publishers
199 W 8th Ave, Suite 3
Eugene, OR 97401

It Happened in Hanoi
By Anley, Vernon L.
Copyright © 2017 by Anley, Vernon L. All rights reserved.
Softcover ISBN-13: 979-8-3852-3320-5
eBook ISBN-13: 979-8-3852-3322-9
Publication date 9/16/2024
Previously published by Mirador Publishing, 2017

This edition is a scanned facsimile of the original edition published in 2017.

By the same author:

A Carnival of Lies
A Divided Universe
An Unholy Love
The Orange Tree and Other Stories

It is a sign of a soldier to believe that there is nothing left of man after death except a corpse.

-ERASMUUS

In killing You changed death to life.

Living Flame, Stanza 2

1

Angel slept intermittently during the non-stop 14 hours flight from Heathrow to Hanoi's Noi Ba airport. His six foot five frame did not sit comfortably in economy seating. Used to flying in military transport aircraft and Black Hawk helicopters, he had not reckoned on a narrow seat pitch that kept him doubled up for most of the flight.

When the plane landed Angel let the other passengers disembark before taking his bag from the overhead locker and leaving the aircraft. Noi Ba reminded him of all the other third world airports he had been in: rundown facilities, and exasperated passengers struggling to follow directions.

Angel gave his passport to an immigration official who became unexpectedly alert when he noticed Angel's height. Told to wait, the man disappeared into a back room with Angels' passport. The immigration officer returned several minutes later accompanied by a security guard. Angel had been arraigned before by border police in Africa who had not been told that the SAS were carrying out anti-terrorist operations in their area. But this was Hanoi and he had a tourist visa. There was no reason for supposing that he had entered the country illegally.

Angel was led to an office adjoining the baggage hall. It was an airless room with a plain wooden table and several plastic chairs. Angel asked his escort if he spoke English. The man shook his head. He wore a leather holster holding a Smith &

Weston K-38 revolver used by the Americans during the Vietnamese War. It was the wrong weapon for airport security. Reloading the chamber with loose rounds can take a painfully long time, even impossible for the novice under stress. Security had not done its homework.

After a few minutes they were joined by a woman wearing a Border Defence uniform, her epaulettes adorned with three gold stars and a stripe. Undaunted by Angel's height she looked directly up into his face and without prefatory talk told Angel that the Head of Security would like to see him. She spoke good English, dropping only the final consonants when she spoke quickly. Her explanation carried a tinge of apology, suggesting that she had not been told the reason for his detention.

'We have a car waiting for you, Mr. Angel. If you give me the name of your hotel we will take care of your luggage.'

There was a time when Angel might have asked for an explanation or called for consular support. But he had long since learned that the best way to deal with these situations was to accept them without complaint. Few things irritated officialdom more than rightful anger.

When Angel resigned from the SAS he could have gone anywhere in Southeast Asia. Most of the countries squeezed between the Indian and the Pacific ocean offered inexpensive living, and a chance to start a new life. Had he stayed in England he might have got a job as a security guard, patrolling shopping malls or escorting VIP's, which many SAS did after retirement. But it was not a path he wished to follow. He had spent too many years responding to the contingencies of the moment without regard to other considerations. What these other consideration were was left unanswered, but their absence was felt as an absence of purpose.

His decision to go to Vietnam was the result of a chance meeting with James Kealy, a retired war correspondent for AAP (Australian Associated Press) in the bar of the Union Jack Club in Sandell Street.

'I accompanied the first Australian troops to Vietnam in June, 1965,' Kealy said. 'We would not have gone to war if America had not gone to war first. We were told that Australia had to build up credits with the U.S to ensure our security. But Communism was never a threat to Australian security. At that time U.S. foreign policy was driven by what Eisenhower called the 'domino' theory. He believed the whole region, including Australia and New Zealand, would collapse to the communists if they won in Vietnam.

'Ho Chi Minh was not a pawn of the Chinese seeking to conquer neighbouring territories as the Americans thought. His only aim was the unification of Vietnam. The attempt to 'contain' China by holding back the North Vietnamese was one of the most disastrous mistakes in the history of warfare. It cost the lives of sixty thousands Americans and more than a million Vietnamese.'

Kealy had long since given up being a war correspondent, but not from writing. Now in his eighties, he had just finished a book on Australia's involvement in the Vietnamese war. Critical of the Australian and American decision to go to war, he was positive about Vietnam and its people.

'When I first went to Saigon, or Ho Chi Minh City as it is now called, it was still a provincial capital – its churches, stucco villas, and tree lined streets the remnants of a century of French colonial presence. Driving through the heat and humidity of a tropical morning I caught my first glimpse of a land still unmarked by war. Peasants in black pyjamas and conical straw hats bent over rice stalks in flooded fields. Temple and pagodas ringed by frangipani trees. Villages alive with ducks and pigs, children riding their pet buffaloes, endless rice fields and swathes of water palm.

'Nobody could have imagined then that three million Americans would serve in Vietnam – and thousands perish in the in the jungles and rice fields. Nor could one have imagined the holocaust that would devastate the country. In the subsequent sixteen years of war 10 percent of the entire populating were killed or wounded. And for what? To bear witness to America's confidence in its military invincibility? The 60,000 names listed on the Vietnam War Memorial in Washington record more than the lives lost in battle: they represent a sacrifice to a failed crusade.'

Kealy spent more time in Vietnam than most correspondents because he was one of only two journalists employed by AAP to cover the war. His most vivid memories were those of Saigon after the arrival of American troops.

'Saigon became a centre of profiteering. Its bars were drug centres, its hotels brothels, its boulevards and squares a sprawling back market hawking everything from sanitary napkins to rifles – all of it purloined from American warehouses. Soldiers, their pockets filled with cash, strolled streets crowded with whores and pimps. Beggars, orphans, cripples, and other victims of devastation. South Vietnamese army generals, enriched by silent Chinese partners, possessed gaudy villas not far from putrid slums packed with refugees. Government officials and businessmen connived constantly, shuffling and reshuffling the seemingly limitless flow of dollars. It was a city for sale – obsessed by greed, oblivious to its impending doom.

'To make the war more palatable the army added 'sweeteners' to its personnel policy. No American serviceman had to stay in Vietnam for more than a year. The 'RTD' or rotation date was on the mind of everyone from the day he stepped off the plane in Saigon. Another carrot was 'R & R', a five day 'rest and relaxation' from the war during a tour of duty. It made the Asian politicians and business men just as happy as the GIs. Foreign ministers from half the countries in the Pacific basin bribed American officials to get their cities approved as 'R& R' sites. As soon as a city won an R&R designation, Government ministers brought up land and set up construction companies. Hundreds of Western-style hotels went up overnight all over Asia – structures that couldn't pass a building inspection without a bribe.

'The GIs were taken to a city of their choice, carrying with them thousands of dollars. Depending on the popularity of the city, from one to five plane loads of servicemen arrived at their destination of choice every week, representing more than a million dollars in free, no-strings attached foreign aid. Pleasure haunts like Bangkok and Hong Kong made $100 million a year from visits by Vietnam-based GIs.

'The biggest R&R business was prostitution, never a negligible business in Asia. During the French war, organized vice had been confined to the Saigon suburb of Chlon, where the Chinese mafia directed casinos, brothels, and opium dens. The French, sensitive to male fragility, maintained the *Bordel Militaire de Campagne*, a brothel that travelled with the troops. But the Americans were too puritanical to sanction sex officially. Tawdry bars and nightclubs and 'massage parlours' proliferated. The local underworld, mostly run by the Chinese, combed the countryside to make offers to ignorant and starving rural families.

Hungry peasants 'sold' excess daughters for a few dollars. Once settled in R&R hotels, steam bath houses and red light districts their lives became one of abortions and abuse.'

Kealy paused for a minute.

'It was a different story when the war ended. The American departure brought the economy to its knees. Cash-strapped, the regime could not meet its military payroll. Wages went unpaid. Malpractice in the army, always a hotbed of corruption, ran wild. Soldiers from the highest levels on down embezzled funds, rice and supplies, stole payrolls and profited from illegal dealings. Girls lined the streets waiting for pick-ups that would never happen. Children pestered you for money, like they always did, but where they had once been Vietnamese, now they were bastard Americans, born of Vietnamese mothers. Vietnamese children of mixed blood stand out in a crowd. Jeered at for their 'strange' looks, they were rejected for being of mixed blood. Many were abandoned by their mothers who were shunned for prostituting themselves. Every Vietnamese city had its colony of mixed-blood orphans living on the streets.'

Angel knew the consequences of war. He had seen blood running form the wounded, and men coughing out their lungs. He had seen the dead lying in mud, their bodies amputated by shrapnel, and limping exhausted men emerge from battle trying to regain their sanity. He had seen towns and villages destroyed. He had seen starving children, and the agony of mothers and wives. Whichever side may call itself the victor, there are no winners in war. All are losers.

'If the war left Saigon relatively unscathed,' Kealy continued, 'the same could not be said for Hanoi. The biggest ever bombing campaign by B-52's took place over Hanoi.

50,000 civilians are said to have died. We had reports of children blinded by rocket fragments and paralysed by machine gun bullets begging for food. Others set on fire by napalm lay dying in the streets. Napalm burns at a thousand degrees Celsius, ten times more than boiling water. It sticks to the flesh and burns through to the bone: the burns fester into a viscous black magma resembling tar. You may have seen the photo of the 9 year old girl running naked, her arms flaying to relive the pain of her burning flesh. She was just one of 100,000 children that needed reconstructive surgery. Only a few of the lucky ones received attention. Those wounded by napalm and not killed outright carry huge scars on their back and arms where napalm sheared off layers of skin.'

Kealy faced Angel and asked, 'What do you know about Ho Chi Minh?'

'Very little.' Angel was ten years old when Kealy first went to Vietnam, and eighteen in 1973 when the war ended. 'The war was not reported widely in the U.K. because the then Prime Minister, Harold Wilson, declined to send troops to Vietnam. I don't remember Ho's name being mentioned.'

'Ho Chi Minh might have died fifty years ago, but the country still lives under his shadow. The introduction of *doi moi* in 1986, Vietnam's equivalent of Perestroika, has moved Vietnam towards a market economy. But don't be misled. Ho's Marxist legacy is still the rule. If you stay in Vietnam for any length of time you will come to his attention of the *Công an Nhân dân Viê* or security service. '

'Why?'

'It holds all strings. As far as the man on the street is concerned, Vietnam's security service is the CPV (Communist Party of Vietnam). It is not subject to the rules and limitations one might expect from a governmental office. It operates on an entirely different principle from that of the civil administration. It makes no concession to the existing legal system. Kai's men can pull you in without reason or apology.'

Angel smiled. 'My warring days are over. I'm not interested in politics. The last thing I want is to get involved with Vietnam's Security Service.'

'Maybe so. But if I give you a sketch of what the Vietnamese call 'the American War' it will help explain why Viet Kai and his colleagues in the politburo keep a stranglehold on the country.

'The Vietnamese saw the war against America and its South Vietnamese ally as the continuation of two thousand years of resistance to Chinese, and later, French rule. Obsessed by a fanatical dedication to a reunified Vietnam the communists were prepared to accept limitless causalities to attain their objective. Ho Ch Minh made that plain to the French as they braced for war in the late 1940s. "You can kill ten of my men for every one I kill of yours; but even at those odds, you will lose and I will win." It is something that the Americans never understood.

'Following the catastrophic defeat of the French by the Viet Minh in 1954 and their withdrawal from Vietnam, a peace agreement divided the country in two parts. Ho Chi Minh took control north of the 17th parallel and Emperor Bao Dai, installed as head of state by the French, held sway south of the parallel. The Geneva Accords stipulated that the division was temporary pending a nationwide election to be held in the summer of 1956.

'The election was never held. Ngo Diem, who ousted Bao Dia with America's backing, refused to hold a general election. He knew that the majority of the population favoured a united

Vietnam under Communists rule. The Americans, having supported Diem, turned a blind eye to the promises made at Geneva, which might otherwise have led to a united Vietnam under Communism.

'President Kennedy could have vetoed any suggestion to get involved in South Vietnam. Instead he chose to go to war, urged on by his advisors to confront Soviet expansionism in Southeast Asia.

'Beginning in late 1963 the flow of American troops and material increased. Kennedy launched the first air strikes against the North, camouflaged as training exercises for Vietnamese pilots, dropping bombs from South Vietnamese aircraft, firing rockets from South Vietnamese helicopters and spraying herbicide defoliants to deny the enemy jungle cover and food. American military participation was kept secret because it was in direct violation of the 1964 Geneva Accords, partitioning North and South Vietnam, to which the United States was a signatory.

Facilitated by a resolution approved by Congress which allowed Lyndon Johnson (who became president after Kennedy's assassination) to escalate military -involvement in Vietnam without a formal declaration of war, he embarked on a bombing campaign to compel Ho to abandon his guerrilla war in the South with the aim of overthrowing Diem and reuniting Vietnam. The bombing campaigns against the North were the longest and heaviest aerial bombardment in history. Flights of B-52, more than 100 bombers at a time, dropped nearly eight million tons of explosives, four times more than was dropped on Nazi Germany in World War II. Such a strategy necessarily involved the massive destruction of human life. But, no matter, said the U.S. Commander-in- Chief, General Westmorland, because, "The Oriental doesn't put the same high price on life as does a Westerner. Life is plentiful, life is cheap in the Orient".

Kealy shook his head, still amazed that Westmorland could have uttered such a crass remark.

'From 1964 until 1973,' Kealy continued, 'when the last U.S. troops left Vietnam, America turned much of Vietnam into a 'free fire zone' with the intention of crushing a peasant army by the profligate use of explosives and herbicides. It was a decade of massive, intentional destruction of both the natural and human ecologies of the country on a scale hitherto unseen in warfare.

'The outcry following the Tet offensive, a massive action launched against the South at the start of the Vietnamese Tet national holiday, pushed Nixon and Kissinger into negotiating a peace with the Communists. 85,000 communist troops surged into more than 100 cities and towns, including Saigon where they broke into the U.S. embassy. Militarily, Tet was a failure for the Viet Cong because it failed to achieve its objective of sparking a revolt against the Saigon regime. But the political impact of Tet was disastrous for the U.S. government. Stunned by images of dead GI's beamed into the living rooms of 50 million Americans each evening destroyed the credibility of government reports that the war was being won. Symbolically more damaging was the assault, on the first day of the offensive, on their supposedly invulnerable embassy in Saigon. By the time the compound had been cleared, five Americans had died – and with them the popular conviction that the war would soon be over.

'By 1967, a massive anti-war movement had taken shape all across the United States. Anti-war demonstrations rocked

American university campuses and spilled onto the streets. People from all sorts of political, social, racial, and religious backgrounds united around the demand for the immediate withdrawal of U.S. troops and an end to American intervention in the war. Eight Americans publicly burnt themselves to death in protest, and thousands were arrested in one day during a demonstration of half a million people. At one such demonstration at Kent State University, national guardsmen fired shots into the crowd, killing four protestors – an action that spurred 100,000 demonstrators to gather in Washington. The violence of the Vietnam War was now spilling onto American streets.

'It was a similar story in Australia. Mounting casualties, rising taxes, and especially the feeling that there was no end in view, changed the public's attitude towards the war. TV news and photos were meant to show the might of the US army, but instead we saw that massive fire power being used against unarmed peasants. We watched civilians fleeing from napalm, charred bodies of Buddhist monks, and the bloodied bodies of villagers slaughtered in American "search and destroy" missions. When news of the My Lai massacre surfaced, 'wharfies' took action, refusing to load a ship carrying military supplies to Vietnam. On July 4, American Independence Day, hundreds of people rallied outside the US embassy in Melbourne, waving Viet Cong flags and chanting, "BJ, how many babies have you killed today" and "One, two, three, four, we don't want your f---ing war".

'The loss of public confidence in winning the war seeped through the ranks of the American armed forces. Its most serious symptom a growing narcotics addiction. Petty drug dealers fronting for senior South Vietnamese government officials supplied the troops with anything they wanted. Ten dollars would buy a vial of pure heroin. You could trade a couple of bars of soap for a carton of marijuana cigarettes soaked in opium. Almost everybody, including officers, were 'doing heroin'. Respect for authority among the GIs broke down. 'Fragging' (fragmentation grenade attacks by men against their officers) become wide spread. As one soldier told me, "Grenades left no fingerprints. Nobody's going to go to jail." By the end of the war 730 officers had been murdered, and these were only the recorded deaths.

'As moral deteriorated U.S. commanders knew that the answer to the problem was to end the war and repatriate the GI's, for whom the conflict had become as pointless as it had for the rest of the American people. Together with the demonstrations and protests, and an upcoming presidential election, Kissinger was driven to strike a deal with Ho Chi Minh's representatives in Paris. As a practical arrangement, at least for Saigon's security, the peace agreement was badly flawed. The Saigon regime and the Viet Cong would continue as distinct entities. Unlike the Geneva agreement signed in 1954, which required the communists to regroup in the north, the Paris agreement allowed both northern and southern forces to remain in the areas each controlled. The breakthrough elated Kissinger, but was ridiculed by his own staff. With 150,000 Viet Cong in South Vietnam, Ho was not going to pull back. When this was pointed out to Kissinger he exploded, "You don't understand. I want to meet their terms. I want to reach an agreement. It can be done, and it will be done. What do you want us to do? Stay there forever?" '

'Kissinger got his way. A peace treaty was signed in 1973 between the U.S. and North Vietnam. For this fudged deal,

Kissinger and Le Duc, Ho's representative, were awarded the Nobel Peace prize, though only Kissinger accepted. To mollify Saigon, the Pentagon arranged for some $2 billion worth of weapons and aircraft to be shipped to South Vietnam, giving the regime the fourth largest air force in the world. But the absence of the B-52s and American advisors meant that it would take years before the ill trained demoralized South Vietnam troops were capable of taking advantage of their superior firepower.

'For the Americans the war was over. The last U.S. prisoners were freed by their North Vietnamese captors at Gia Lam airport a few months after the treaty was signed. But for Ho Chi Minh the treaty merely marked a new phase of the war. With the Americans out of the way, he pursued his objective of uniting Vietnam – a task made easier by Nixon going back on his written assurance that the US would intervene militarily in support of South Vietnam if the communists renewed their offensive.

'By March 1975 the northern half of South Vietnam was under Ho's control. A month later American and pro-American Vietnamese began a race against time to evacuate Saigon. Over a span of eighteen hours, shuttling back and forth between the city and a flotilla of ships and aircraft carriers riding offshore, a fleet of seventy marine choppers lifted more than a thousand Americans and nearly six thousand Vietnamese out of the beleaguered capital from the seventh-floor rooftop of the US embassy. The last helicopter left the embassy just minutes before an NVA tank crashed through the gates of the South Vietnamese presidential palace. Finally, all of former French Indochina – Vietnam, Cambodia, and Laos – was under communist rule.'

'And the aftermath?' Angel asked.

'That's another story. It is not a happy one, but then

anything to do with war rarely is. The Southerners eyed the future with apprehension, and their fears were well founded. Hanoi was in no mood to grant Saigon autonomy: the Council of National Reconciliation, provided by the Paris Accords, was never established. The impression of a conquering army was exacerbated when northern cadres swarmed south to take up all official posts. Bitterness on Hanoi's part towards its former enemies was inevitable; yet instead of making moves towards national conciliation, and despite the fact that many families had connections in both camps, recriminations drove further wedges between the peoples of north and south.'

'You don't paint a happy picture,' Angel said.

'I'm talking historically. Although the past is not forgotten, and the years following post-reunification are a stain on the history of the CPV, the enmity has largely disappeared. What has not disappeared, and is still alive for the leadership, is the price the country paid to free itself from colonial oppression.'

Kealy was silent, and then said, 'If you are thinking of going to Vietnam you won't be disappointed. It is the best and cheapest place to live in Southeast Asia. If you don't mind some communist flag waving, and keep your nose clean, it's a great place to live. You won't need a car, and you won't need a credit card. You'll find life a lot quieter and simpler than in the West.'

It is surprising how often, during the most critical moments of life, everything hangs on chance. Angel's meeting with Kealy was one such occasion. Unsure of his next move, Kealy had pointed Angel in the direction of Vietnam. As for the *Công an Nhân dân Việt Nam* and Viet Kai, it never crossed Angel's mind that their paths would cross.

2

Angel had lived with his parents until he was eighteen in a small end of terrace house on the outskirts of London. He was an only child, his parents being in their late thirties when they married. Angel was never sure that his birth was intended, not because he was without siblings, but because his parents lived their own secret life which he was never fully a part of. They received scarcely any visitors, never ate a meal away from home, and never spent an evening with friends. At night they read aloud to one another, or listened to the radio. A stranger might think they lived a life of loneliness and deprivation, but their contentment was complete and unfeigned.

Angel, used to being on his own, learned to entertain himself without intervention from others. He had few friends, and few outdoor amusements. This is not to say that laughter and play were absent from his life. There were certain stock family jokes which seldom failed to enliven the breakfast table. Nor was solitary play a hardship. He enjoyed making his own rules and not having to meet other people's expectations.

His parents lived in an atmosphere of faith. As long as their lives were not clouded by sin, to which they were delicately sensitive, they took the passing hour lightly. Every Sunday Angel dutifully accompanied his parents to the local Methodist church. He sang hymns of praise and humiliation, without questioning the reality of the person to whom they were addressed.

At the age of twelve Angel was the tallest boy in his class. It was sufficient reason to be chosen to take the part of Themistocles in *The Persian War* Angel took the role of the Athenian general to heart, allowing his imagination to look beyond the exigencies of a stage and a cast played by actors. History became his favourite subject, encouraged by a present from his parents of a set of metal toy soldiers engaged in the Battle of Waterloo. While placing the opposing armies on his bedroom floor he saw that Napoleon could have won the war by storming the British positions without waiting to use his artillery. This would have allowed Napoleon to check the British advance before the arrival of Von Blucher's Prussians. When Angel moved his armies the images they raised in his mind were of real people, moving in open air, in a battle of real engagement. Angel revealed a precocious ability to see accurately and pursue a strategy based on opportunity. A gift quickly recognized later by the army and the SAS.

Angel's parents died within a few weeks of each other. In death, as in life, they took their last journey together in the full knowledge of their immediate reunion. Angel felt sadness and loss, but accepted their passing without tears. He had always thought himself to be an accessory to their marriage, never a prominent part of it. Love was not absent, but it rarely showed itself in acts of affection.

Angel left school and joined the army the year his parent's died. He possessed a self sufficiency that seemed to others a kind of courage in itself. The army saw in Angel a native capacity for leadership, strategic thinking, and self-discipline. After six months he was seconded to the Special Air Services and sent to Sennybridge camp near the Brecon Beacons. After a gruelling selection procedure he received training in close quarter battle skills and counter-terrorist techniques. Although the final score and comments are confidential, Angel was one of only five graduates from several hundred applicants. After earning his SAS wings he was promoted from NCO to officer. Since all SAS officers are ranked captain or above, Angel, aged twenty, was one of the youngest serving officers in the British army.

For the next thirty years Angel saw one theatre of war after another. All were dangerous, and all required a high degree of expertise with assault weapons and explosive devices along with knowledge of terrorist tactics and psychology. Many of these operations were so sensitive that they had no official authorization.

Africa was the principal field of Angel's activity. Bloody struggles for independence, ethnic and tribal differences, and the absence of any meaningful democratic channel for opposition to new regimes made insurgency and civil war inevitable. Anxious African rulers knew that even a small handful of armed men could overthrow a fragile government. Similarly, an equally small number of armed men could prevent or reverse it. The SAS was the first call for the heads of state supported by the British government that feared an armed insurrection.

During nearly three decades of almost continuous combat he had been wounded only once. Although the SAS were trained to infiltrate within a few hundred yards of a closely guarded position, changing camouflage up to half a dozen times as they crossed different areas of ground, and then hit the target without being seen, things did not always go to plan. Angel had pinpointed a rebel stronghold in the hills near Azare in Northern Nigeria when an undisciplined body of government troops broke cover and opened fire starting a fire-fight with the enemy. Angel tried to keep the fighting away from the civilian population by redirecting the fire when he was hit in the chest. Shot by an AK-47, the force of the impact was like a hammer blow. As Angel fell to the ground he felt his life slipping away, a transitional death before the absolute end.

The SAS never abandon a wounded man, but if a patrol member is killed, he is left behind. As soon as there was a lull in the fighting, a fellow SAS checked Angel's pulse. Seeing that Angel was alive he arranged for him to be taken out by helicopter to the government hospital in Kano. In a matter of days he was airlifted to the Queen Elizabeth Hospital in Birmingham, the main receiving unit for all military patients injured overseas.

While Angel was convalescing he recalled the bullet's impact, and descent into unconsciousness. Aware of a deathless element within himself, he had felt himself elevated into a dimension beyond earthly consciousness. There is no fixed rule of antecedence for such an experience. It may be compacted into the moment of a blinded Saul falling from his horse on the way to Damascus, or extended over the slow maturing process of a lifetime. For Angel the epiphany was as sudden as it was revelatory. The apprehension confounded his understanding of life and man's place in the universe.

God and immortality had not been among Angel's concerns. The magnet of meaning was always the present: the immediacy of life and death. He did not attend church services hoping that by example he would inspire his men to believe that God was on their side. It did not make sense to talk of God to a soldier whose business it was to cut throats. The overriding determinate was not to let down the men who stood beside you. The spiritual aspects of being had no place when reality was the bomb blast and rifle fire.

The realization of life's value, its singular uniqueness and permanence, rejected the pessimism with which Angel had accepted violence and warfare as inevitable. Life and death were not mere matters of fact, but an invitation to higher orders of experience.

Angel had never fought for personal or individual reasons, such as anger, revenge, or fame; and those he had come up against, terrorists or professional soldiers had, like himself, made a general commitment to violence. To survive, psychically, one had to step outside conventional conduct and come to terms with the guilt of killing and maiming people.

Angel told Kealy that his 'warring days were over'. The years spent searching out terrorists in mountains, jungles and marshes now appeared counter-productive in realizing the social and political ends they were supposed to achieve. Killing, which in the field was both necessary and obligatory, was not simply the outcome of ill will, mistrust and fear. There was a theological dimension to man's readiness to violence that he had not realized before. Man's link with the eternal affirmed the sacredness of life. Killing was not merely a *cul-de-sac* for human progress, it was a stain on man's essential being.

After leaving hospital Angel was offered an administrative post in SAS HQ in Credenhill, Herefordshire. The work involved record keeping and the financial accountability of operational sections. He became so bored that he resigned after a month.

Many soldiers who left the SAS became mercenaries, in spite of the U.N. Convention which bans their use. The SAS had given Angel the needed reward for a life in pursuit of action. The more exertion is called upon, as in battle, the more one partakes in the direct tang of living, wholly apart from the end achieved. But when the intensity of combat had lost its thrall, war, for all its activity, become empty of meaning.

3

There are more than ten million motorbikes in Vietnam. All of them, it seemed to Angel, were on the airport road into Hanoi. No one obeyed traffic signals or lights. Motorbikes, with as many as five people riding pavilion, pushed their way through the traffic, horns hooting. The impression was one of total anarchy and chaos.

Thirty people a day are killed in traffic accidents in Vietnam, putting the country in the top ten of road fatalities in the world. The law requires everyone to wear helmets, but it is never enacted because people refused to comply – perhaps the only time in Vietnam's history that a government edict had been ignored.

It took nearly an hour, past the rubble of building sites, gaudy billboards and the shanties on the outskirts of Hanoi to reach the huge multi-storey VPPS (Vietnam People's Public Security) Headquarters in Phan Van Dong Street. The looming building was one that Angel would get to know well over the coming months. Its faceless exterior concealed a web of corridors and closed doors behind which 4000 police and security officers keep tabs on every man, woman and child in Vietnam.

Angel was taken to an office on the twelfth floor bearing the gold star emblem of the Ministry of Public Security. After a short wait he was admitted into a spacious room with a large

French partner's desk, several comfortable arm chairs and a tall double bookshelf holding leather bound volumes of Karl Marx's collected works. Black and white photographs of the Vietnam War hung on the walls. On a clothes' rack was a *khăn rằn*, the traditional chequered black and white scarf worn by the Viet Cong during the war.

Standing behind the desk was Major General Viet Kai, Head of Vietnam's Communist-controlled state security apparatus and senior member of the Politburo. Angel and Kai looked at one another. Angel, at ease, and more observant than his relaxed manner would suggest, stood head and shoulders above the Security Chief. Kai, impeccably dressed, wore civilian clothes. His dark grey suit was tailor made in the English style, slim fit and double breasted. Tall for a Vietnamese, but still a head shorter than Angel, he had deep set eyes which were set off by a high forehead and thick white hair. Angel guessed that Kai was in his mid sixties or early seventies, old enough to have taken part in the Battle of Ia Drang Valley, the first major encounter between the U.S. Army and the NVA.

Answerable only to Kai, the departments under the Minister's control employed 6.7 million Vietnamese, roughly one-sixth of its 43-million working population. Ranked number two in the Politburo after the General Secretary of the Central Committee, Viet Kai was the most powerful government official in Vietnam. Kai gestured to the chair in front of his desk and asked Angel to sit down. Angel's line of sight was above Kai's head, on the same level as the photographs of Kai leading patrols along the banks of the Me Kong or one of the tributaries that cross the DMZ. Angel waited for Kai to speak. Kai introduced himself by name, omitting his rank and title, a concession Angel acknowledged with a nod of his head.

'What brings you to Vietnam, Mr. Angel?'

'I'm on vacation.'

'Nothing more?'

'No.' There was much more, but it was none of Kai's business. Angel was not about to tell Kai that a series of events had undermined the credibility of his life with the SAS.

'Mr. Angel,' Kai continued, 'we will need to detain you for a short time, but the inconvenience will be minimal.'

'Why?'

Kai ignored the question. 'Your passport photograph shows you in uniform.'

'Yes.'

'There are many gaps and irregular entries. I presume these omissions are combat related?'

'I was with the SAS. We served in many places, sometimes at very short notice.'

'Then you have been trained to identify targets and kill them?'

'SAS operations often involve the taking of life.'

'You were a marksman?'

'Yes.'

Kai paused. 'If you were to assassinate someone, what would be your weapon of choice?'

A strange question, but Angel answered in the same matter of fact voice. 'Short range, the Russian SV.22.'

'And for a target over 100 yards?'

'You have a number of choice.'

Kai reached behind his desk and took down an M16 from a gun rack and passed it to Angel. 'This rifle?'

'It's not a sniper's rifle. But yes, it would do.'

'Did you know Mr. Angel, that these rifles are readily available in Vietnam?'

'I'm not surprised,' Angel said, returning the rifle. 'It was standard issue for the Americans fighting here.' Angel paused, and then said, 'Mr. Kai, are you suggesting that I came to Vietnam to assassinate someone?'

'Why did you come to Vietnam, Mr Angel?'

'I told you. I'm on vacation.'

'But you are not adverse to killing when necessary.'

On Angel's first mission with the SAS he came face to face with a UNITA guerrilla. Angel saw in the man's eyes another human being like himself, and simultaneously saw the man's body torn apart as he applied pressure to his trigger finger. Everything happened in a split-second. Life and death and no in-between. There was no time for reflection. The beauty of war. It made killing easier.

'I was with the SAS, Mr. Kai. We fought against terrorist organizations and armed militants. As long as such groups are in the field government forces will take military action against them.'

'Would you include Marxist guerrilla groups among the insurgents and terrorists?'

'Yes.'

'Are you aware, Mr. Angel, that Vietnam is a communist country? That we uphold Ho Chi Minh's Marxist values? That your government and the Americans regard the Viet Cong as insurgents?

'That was a long time ago.'

'Not so long Mr. Angel. Relations were not normalized until 1995. Many senior members of the Party served with the National Liberation Front.'

'No one disputes that the Communist Party is the ruling political party of Vietnam.'

'There are two million people in Vietnam's Communist Party. Two million out of a population of 83 million. You will appreciate, Mr. Angel, that we are in the minority. We have our critics in various spheres of public life – economic, cultural, religious. We have been able to contain those hostile to the Party, but we must be vigilant.'

'I have nothing against the CPV.'

Kay ignored the interjection. 'Some people will go to any lengths to destabilize the government: assassination, arson, sabotage. The very activities, Mr. Angel, that you excel in.'

'Mr. Kai,' Angel said, with a touch of weariness, 'I have nothing against your government. And I am not here at the request of anyone hostile to the regime.'

The interrogation was a surreal distortion of the facts, but not without its danger. Kai could suspend all normally respected procedures if he chose to.

'You realise, Mr. Angel, that you possess certain skills we do not normally welcome.'

Angel looked at the black and white photographs behind Kai's head. More dangerous to the Americans than the aircraft and weapons supplied to the NVA (North Vietnamese Army) by China and the Soviet Union were the Viet Cong patrols led by men like Kai. The Viet Cong were virtually undetectable, an enemy in the shadows. Each fighter was a model of adaptability and efficiency. They carried Kalashnikovs on their backs, carefully attached so as not to slip round or flip over; cartridge clips and grenades hanging from their webbing; sacks of rice tied to their stomachs and a waterproof canvas for sleeping in the rain.

Nearly all 48,000 U.S. combat deaths were at the hands of the Viet Cong.

Angel did not reply to Kai's question. In joining the SAS he had consciously embarked on a mode of life which involved killing other people. He had become an assenting party to what was required of him and took full responsibility for the obligations placed upon him. As a soldier, the important thing was to know what was demanded of you, not the virtue of any code governing human relationships. Kai knew this. He also knew that one could leave the past behind.

'Mr. Kai,' Angel said, 'I've had a long flight. If you have no objection I would like to go to my hotel now. You know where I am staying if you need see me again.'

Angel did not raise his voice, but got to his feet.

'Very well, Mr. Angel. There are a few things we need to clear up. In the mean time you may go to your hotel. One of my men will stay with you, but he will be discreet.' And then, in a more friendly voice, 'To make your stay more agreeable I will arrange for one of our guides to show you our city. You are fortunate to be here at the time of the *Yen Tu* festival. Perhaps you would like to participate in the Blessing ceremony, where you can pray for your security and good health.'

4

Angel's hotel, the Bao Ninh, was in Hanoi's Old Quarter. It was a 'tube' (or tunnel) building, so-called because of its narrow frontage. The style dates back to the Le Dynasty (1428-1788), when they were popular as a way of limiting the property tax which was based on the width of the building. Confined to the ground area by the original land deeds, owners have had to expand upwards, creating four, or five-story buildings on plots that are only a few meters wide.

Angel had not slept for forty eight hours. But sleep did not come easily. He was uncomfortable with Kai's interrogation. Its purpose was not clear. Kai was the sole authority for all police matters. His executive powers allowed him to ignore existing rules and legislation. He could expel or detain Angel indefinitely without explanation. The only way to oppose a decision made by the Security Police was to make a disciplinary complaint (an illusory means of redress because in the last instance that complaint was dealt with by the Police themselves).

The breakfast room the next morning was empty but for some American tourists having a last minute coffee while waiting for the airport bus. Angels' minder was seated on a leather sofa next to the entrance watching a choir of men in army uniforms on TV singing against painted backdrops of peach blossoms. The man was in plain clothes, and unarmed.

As soon as he saw Angel he got to his feet and introduced himself. Lung Van spoke in broken English. In his early forties, he had a pale face, straight black hair and watchful eyes. His speech and movement were deliberate and considered, almost as if he were the one, not Angel, that was being observed.

Angel had given little thought to his surveillance, assuming that Kai would realize his mistake soon enough. He would have dismissed the events of yesterday had he not been interviewed by Kai. Cases of mistaken identity or illegal entry are normally dealt with by airport security, not by the Head of Security. If Kai had grounds for thinking that Angel had been recruited by an enemy of the State there would be no redress or court of appeal. Kealy had made clear that Kai required no legal backing for any action he might take.

There were many Vietnamese who would happily see the end of Communism as Kai had said. The Party's Marxist ideology did not tolerate the development of political ideas at variance with its ideology. That morning the Hanoi *Times* quoted a speech by Thái Bình, the Interior Minister, in which he blamed foreigners for 'fermenting virulent attacks against Marxism-Leninism and the party's leadership'. Strip away the party line, and it was clear that the 'virulent attacks' were a protest against the corruption, inept leadership and the high living standards of senior commissioners. In all probability there was a revolutionary infrastructure in Vietnam, particularly in large urban areas such as Hanoi or Ho Chi Minh City. But there was nothing in Angel's past that could link him to any opposition movement. If detention should lead to arrest, it was not because there were grounds for custody, but because the Party was so unsure of its legitimacy that it saw danger where none existed.

After leaving Security Headquarters Angel had considered calling the British Embassy, but his experience with embassy staff abroad was less than encouraging. While with the SAS he had been obliged to liaise with consular officials before carrying out cross border incursions. On each occasion plans had to be approved by a hierarchy of officials who, because they feared making a mistake, postponed taking a decision. It would be the same in Vietnam. The embassy would decline to ask for the return of his passport or protest against his surveillance. They would advise patience, and wait for the outcome of Kai's investigation, no matter how long it might take.

When Angel finished breakfast Luong Van introduced him to Madam Hu, his guide. She was a slim, middle aged woman, with sharp eyes, who spoke good English with a faint American accent. Madam Hu and the driver sat in the front of the small black Peugeot. Angel, his knees bent double, sat squeezed in the back next to Luong Van.

As soon as they were seated Madam Hu began extolling the virtues of the Communist Party. She presented her facts with a tight-lipped earnestness that dared Angel to contradict her.

'The VCP was founded by Ho Chi Minh in 1930,' she said. 'We are one of only four communist countries left in the world; China, Cuba, and North Korea being the others. Vietnam is a socialist republic with a one-party system led by the Communist Party. The party believes that socialism leads to human liberation from exploitation and injustice, etc.'

Since the Vietnamese are neither independent nor free, and that any political idea at variance with the will of the Party is regarded as subversive, the idea of Vietnam being a beacon of 'liberation' was communist spin that only the likes of Madam

Hu could utter without an apologetic smile. Madam Hu continued her eulogy of the Communist Party until they reached Ho Chi Minh's mausoleum, the most important 'sight' on her agenda.

Although Angel had no particular interest in Ho Chi Minh or his mausoleum (a facsimile of Lenin's tomb in Moscow) it was impossible not to be impressed by the enormous black stone edifice that is Ho's final resting place. The mausoleum, built to house Ho's body encased in a glass sarcophagus, was a gift from the Soviet Union. It sits majestically on Hanoi's expansive Ba Dinh Square, the nation's ceremonial epicentre. It was here that Ho declared Vietnam's independence to half a million people in 1945. Ho stated in his will that he did not want a commemorative tomb but that his cremated remains be divided between the north and south of the country with each site marked by a simple shelter. The grandiose building in which he now lies is sadly at odds with his wishes.

'You are lucky,' Madam Hu said, turning to Angel. 'The mausoleum is not always open. Three months each year Ho's embalmed body is flown back to Russia for maintenance.'

The queue to see Ho's corpse was more than 500 meters long (20,000 people visit the mausoleum each week). Madam Hu, disdainful of the stares of those waiting to be admitted, walked straight to the building's entrance. She showed her security pass to the guards, and was immediately ushered forwarded along with Angel and Lung Van.

There were no foreigners in the queue that Angel could see, just Vietnamese, curious to see the leader whom they believed dedicated his life to their welfare, accepting the sacrifice of a lifetime of celibacy. That Ho Chi Minh married, had numerous mistresses and offspring out of wedlock, and refused to see his wife after he became President has been purged from his official biography. So too was his time in the Carlton Hotel whose renowned chef, George Escoffier, promoted him to assistant pastry cook. Other omissions included his time as a monk in Bangkok and his brutal land reforms that resulted in the execution of 13,000 'landlords and reactionaries' – a genocidal purge eclipsed only by the nightmare of the Tet massacres when the Communists under Ho's command slaughtered 8000 civilians in 26 days.

Inside the building's marble entrance hall they were greeted by Ho's most quoted maxim: *Nothing is more important than independence and freedom*. After translating the text Madam Hu led Angel and Lung Van up a broad flight of stairs to the inner sanctum where Ho's embalmed body lies under glass. Ho was dressed in a white Mao jacket, his thin hands clasped to his chest. Angel looked at the waxen face for a few seconds before being ushered forward by jackbooted guards in snow white uniforms. Madam Hu, who must have seen Ho's mortal remains many times, was moved to tears.

Obliged to follow Madam Hu, Angel could not escape seeing more Ho memorabilia: his stilt house, a simple structure with open sides and split-bamboo screens, and Presidential Palace, a beautifully restored French colonial building now used to receive visiting heads of state. It is unlikely that Ho spent much time in either place. It would have been too tempting a target for US bombers had it been known that he was living there.

Ho Chi Minh died in his bed in Hanoi in September 1969 from heart failure, aged 79. News of his death was withheld from the public for nearly 48 hours because he died on the anniversary of his speech in 1945 in which he read out the

Declaration of Independence. The Republic was short lived. The following year, in March 1946, the French reasserted its control over all Indochina.

Determined to forge a united Vietnam, Ho launched a guerrilla war against the French which culminated in the defeat of the French in 1954 at Dien Bien Phu, a remote site in northern Vietnam. Ho Chi Minh's representatives at the peace conference in Geneva were in a strong position to claim independence and the unification of Vietnam. But the French and the Americans, fearing the spread of communism, argued for the division of Vietnam. Compelled to comply with the decision, Ho ignored the cease fire, infiltrating the Viet Cong into south Vietnam. Initially the French were able to contain his guerrillas, but after Mao's communist forces defeated the Nationalists, Mao supported the Viet Cong with additional supplies of arms, turning the tide in Ho's favour. The Americans responded by dropping more than 7 million tons of bombs on Vietnam, more than twice the amount dropped on Europe and Asia during the Second World War

Counted among the casualties of the bombing was the model Quan Lap leper colony. It was bombed not just once, which might have been an accident, but thirty-nine times. Photographs appeared in American papers of doctors and attendants carrying lepers to safety on their backs and on stretches – limbs wasted to stumps, arms ending in knobs. One hundred and sixty secluded buildings were demolished. The surviving lepers were distributed to district and provincial hospitals, placing an addition burden on resources. The motive for bombing a model leper colony? No one could say.

5

Angel was having a nightcap in the hotel bar after dinner when a looming figure entered the dimly lit room. Angel watched the man walk towards him in the mirror behind the bar. Although Angel and the barmaid were the only two people in the room the stranger sat down, uninvited, on the stool alongside him. The man said nothing until he had ordered a double Bau *Da*, a Vietnamese Rice Whisky.

'Mr. Angel?'

Angel turned, and looked into a pair of eyes so expressionless that they might have been made of glass.

'Yes.'

'My name is Aquino.'

Angel guessed from the name and facial features that the man was from the Philippines. Angel guessed that the two deep scars on his forehead were caused by duelling with blades. Aquino was an expert in the martial arts of the Philippines. Arnisadore emphasizes weapon-based fighting with knives and bladed weapons. Aquino could kill with a switchblade as swiftly as he could with a gun.

'You were arrested by the Security Police.' It was not a question.

'Yes.'

'A case of mistaken identity?'

'Most likely.'

'Would it surprise you, Mr. Angel, if I told you that I am the reason for your arrest?'

'Since my arrival I've had nothing but surprises. But yes, it would surprise me. Would you like to explain?'

'In good time Mr. Angel. It's not often that I have the chance to talk to another professional.'

'Another professional?'

'Yes,' Mr. Angel. 'I also kill people.'

'You are referring to my time with the SAS? We did what we had to do.' Angel had said the same thing to Kai. It didn't sound very convincing then, nor did it now when repeated to Aquino.

'People like us,' Aquino continued, 'are different. We don't feel anything for the people we kill. They don't exist for us.'

Aquino's voice was as expressionless as his eyes. It took Aquino's his last remark for Angel to realise that the man beside him was not an anti-communist activist but a pathological killer.

'The killing started with my father. He wore a thick black leather belt with a brass buckle. After he had a few drinks he'd slide it off and strap me until I bled. I hated him.' Aquino paused. 'I was just a kid when he killed my mother. He hit her on the back of the head one too many times and she never got back up. He made me tell everybody that that she had died falling down the stairs. At that time I didn't know what death was. I just knew that my mother was in a wooden coffin that smelled of pine and would not wake up.

'My father was my first victim. I shot him when I was twelve with .38 revolver which I got from a gang member I played pool with. My father spent his time drinking and whoring around Manila's red light district. One night when he got home I put the .38 to his head and pulled the trigger. Boom. One shot to the left side of the head just above the ear. After that, I knew no one could touch me, even if they were bigger than me. I could decide who lived and who died, when and where and how. It made me feel good.'

Angel listened in silence.

'How can I help you Mr. Aquino?' The question seemed strangely banal after listening to Aquino's confession.

'Mr. Angel, there is nothing you can do for me, but I can do something for you. In a couple of days you will be arrested for murder. I suggest you leave Vietnam.'

'Who am I suppose to kill?'

Aquino shook his head. 'You don't need to know.'

'On what evidence?'

'Your fingerprints are all over the M16. It's an old ruse. It's all the evidence Kai needs.'

'What's your connection with Kai?'

'Politics.'

'Politics?'

'Kai is a hard-boiled Marxist. If someone steps out of line, he disappears. It is as simple as that.'

'And you make them 'disappear'.

'That's what I do Mr Angel. I make people disappear.'

'And the next target to disappear.....The one I am supposed to kill?'

'Is a businessman with close ties to the Americans.'

'And his crime?'

'That's Kai's business.'

'Why am I to be arrested for his murder?'

'Kai has his reasons.'

'That's no answer.'

'It's answer enough,'

If Aquino was telling the truth, Angel had become entrapped in a clandestine killing for no reason other than a passing likeness to the assassin.

'Why are you telling me this?'

'I'm paid to kill people, Mr. Angel, not to set them up. Take my advice. Leave the country. You've got no rights here, especially people like you.'

'What do you mean by "people like me"?'

'Your background, Mr. Angel. Vietnam doesn't want people with your experience of revolutionary warfare. Have you heard of the *Viet Tan*?

'No.'

'It is a network of activists inside Vietnam calling for a more democratic form of government. Anyone the Party considers sympathetic to their aims is arrested and sent to a camp in Nghe An. No trial, no appeal, no warrant. He just disappears. There are several revolutionary groups like the *Viet Tan* in Vietnam. You can see why Kai wants to keep his eye on you.'

Aquino took a piece of note paper from his shirt pocket and wrote down a name and an address. 'Lai is a good man,' he said, passing the note to Angel. 'He can help you get out of the country. It will cost you, but not much. I suggest you see him before it is too late.'

Aquino stood up. A big man, as tall as Angel. 'It has been nice talking to you Mr. Angel.'

Angel noticed that Aquino walked quietly on the balls of his enormous feet. Light as a cat for all his bulk. A killer's walk.

6

If he had not heard it from Aquino, Angel would not have believed that Vietnam endorsed State sponsored assassinations. To discover enemies of the State, to watch them and to render them harmless is the preventive duty of the police. In order to fulfil this duty the police must be free to use every means at its disposal, but within legal norms. In Vietnam, the use of such norms was at the discretion of one man, the chief of the Security Service, Major general Viet Kai. Under his leadership the security police had ceased being a defensive instrument for the protection of the State and had become an offensive instrument for the persecution of anyone at odds with the Party.

In all countries the security police have the greatest scope, or at least the most convenient justification, for unauthorized executive measures and deviation from normal rules. Although this state of affairs is not peculiar to communist countries, it is more evident in regimes with a totalitarian power structure. Two Russian security agents were flown into England on Putin's orders to assassinate Alexander Litvinenko using polonium from a Russian state nuclear reactor. And there is a growing belief that Russian assassins, former KGB men, were responsible for the helicopter crash in Dorset which killed Stephen Curtis, who was involved in complex deals over Russian oil.

Among the unanswered questions raised by Aquino was why

he had made himself known to Angel. Contract killers do not reveal their identity. It was easier to believe that Kai was behind the meeting between them than credit Aquino with an altruistic concern for Angel's welfare. Killing had become theatre, creating the illusion of transcending the limitations of human morality: the transformation of impotence into the experience of omnipotence. It was unlikely that Aquino felt any more empathy for Angel than for any of his victims.

Angel dismissed the notion that Kai had ordered his detention because of a passing likeness to a homicidal criminal, although it would suit his purpose to have an offender to take the rap for Aquino if the big man was identified. More likely he had become part of a covert operation known only to Kai. Whatever reason Kai had for keeping his passport, Angel took Aquino's warning seriously. He could seek refuge in the British Embassy; insist on consular support, demanded repatriation. But embassies in Vietnam acceded to the political control and requests of the Communist Party. If an embassy did otherwise it invited displeasure and ultimately suspension. If Kai demanded Angel's custody, the Embassy would oblige as a matter of course. It was a Kafkaesque situation which under normal circumstances translate into comedy, but which in Vietnam was dangerous to ignore.

Angel decided to take Aquino's advice. To leave the country so soon after his arrival was a disappointing start to the hope of finding a more purposeful life than the one left behind. He knew there were aspects of his life that remained unfulfilled, that even the most concentrated fighting had not been able to compensate for.

Angel knew better than most that life could not be taken for granted. For many people the immediate feeling of life touches no limit: to be alive is to expect that each next moment will be followed by another. Angel had known too many moments when there was a real possibility of there being no next moment. This experience led him to deal anxiously with time as infinitely precious. To cancel out his time in Vietnam was a bitter disappointment.

7

Angel waited till after midnight before leaving his room. To avoid disturbing Lung Van, asleep in leather armchair opposite the reception desk, he avoided the lift, walking silently down the staircase to the lobby, through the empty kitchen and into the alley behind the hotel. Even at this late hour the streets were loud and crowded with hawkers selling fake fashion items, DVD's, and other branded items. Despite international criticism and the occasional lawsuit, the copying of almost anything and everything is a major industry in Vietnam.

In the shop-houses selling fake art are paintings from a whole time line of modern art from Impressionism to Op Art. The copies are so skilful that half the paintings in the Fine Arts Museum in Hanoi are said to be 'variants'. Fearing the museum would be destroyed by U.S. bombing raids, museum officials removed hundreds of paintings by Vietnamese artists for safekeeping to the countryside. When these were returned after the war they got mixed up with copies made to replace them. Now it is almost impossible to determine the provenance of many of the thousands of paintings and objects on the walls and in storage.

Angel's attention was not on the Picasso's and Chagall's that spilled out onto the street, but focussed on finding his way through the labyrinth of lanes and streets to the Golden Goat Bar. Lai's bar was so named because the goat is revered in

Vietnam for its sexual prowess. Restaurateurs proclaim the aphrodisiacal qualities of goat meat, and recommend drinking rice wine in a bottle containing a goat's penis to boost sexual performance.

Lai's bar was in a lane lined with small brothels advertising themselves as karaoke bars or massage parlours. Angel was welcomed into the noisy interior by several girls dressed in short skirts and see through tops. Shouting to make himself heard he asked for Mr. Lai and was pointed in the direction of a door behind the dance floor. Lai might have been mistaken for one of his clients. He was young, smart, and wore a gold chain around his neck. As soon as Angel mentioned Aquino's name, Lai grasped the implications of Angel's visit and produced a map of North-Central Vietnam.

'The driver will take you here,' he said pointing to the Cau Treo border. 'It is 400 kilometres from Hanoi, and will take about six hours. The crossing is mostly used by locals, many of them smugglers, carrying contraband items into Vietnam. Give the border guards $20 each. They will wave you through without asking for your passport. From Cau Treo it is just 200 meters to the Laos Border. You can take a bus from there to Vientiane, a five hour ride. The British Embassy is easy to find. It is in the centre of town, opposite the Ptuxay Memorial.'

'And the cost?'

'Five hundred dollars.'

Angel would have preferred a more clandestine route, entering Laos by mountain path, animal trail, or disused crossing. But Lai assured him that illegal crossing into Laos was frequent and trouble free 'The guards will look the other way. They won't even check your suitcase. Very little is smuggled out of Vietnam. It was different during the war. Bodies of American GI's were flown out from Da Nang to Travis Air Force Base in the States. The body bags, and sometimes the bodies themselves were stuffed with heroin. But since the introduction of the death penalty for smuggling drugs contraband now is mostly wildlife.'

Given this assurance, Angel agreed to Lai's terms and arrangements.

Madam Hu and Lung Van were waiting for Angel in the lobby when he came down to breakfast the next morning. Madam Hu wanted to take Angel to see the pagodas adjoining Ho Chi Minh's Palace and the great man's garden which he planted himself. Having had a surfeit of Uncle Ho the day before, and mindful that this was his last day in Hanoi, Angel proposed Halong Bay, a UNESCO world heritage site, as a more attractive alternative. Madam Hu gave a disappointed shrug, conscious that she would have to remain silent during the four hour drive as there were few tributes to Ho en route.

Much of the road to Halong Bay was unpaved, crowded with motorbikes and small trucks, with occasional rice paddies appearing between never-ending roadside shop-houses, stalls, small factories, and pottery kilns. The long drive and interminable traffic was offset by the magical landscape of the Bay itself. One of the seven Natural Wonders of the World, the 2000 jungle-clad limestone islands rise out of the sea like sculptured pieces of jade. Using her security ID Madam Hu appropriated a large timber vessel that looked like a Chinese Junk. Establishing her authority she pointed the Captain in the direction of the 'Grotto of the Heavenly Palace' with its text-book display of sparkling stalactites and stalagmites, supposedly petrified characters of the Taoist Heavenly Court.

For the next few hours the captain guided Madam Hu and Angel through silent secretive channels, past bobbing clusters of fishing boats, hidden bays, overhanging cliffs of ribbed limestone and needle sharp islands. 'Legend has it,' said Madam Hu, 'that a celestial dragon and her children sent by the Jade Emperor to stop a Chinese invasion. The dragons spat out a great number of razor sharp mountains in the path of the enemy fleet. After the victory the dragons, enchanted by their creation, decided to remain, giving rise to the name Ha Long (dragon descending) and to the claimed sighting of sea monsters.'

The enchantment was disfigured by the huge influx of tourism and its consequent problems of litter and pollution. Worsened by the daily activities of people living and conducting their business alongside the Bay, the blue waters of Ha Long are awash with flotsam and slicks of diesel from the huge array of san pans. Madam Hu directed her temper at the hastily erected bamboo stalls at every stopping point selling coral and sea shells stripped from the sea floor, along with fragments of stalagmites and stalactites broken off from caves and grottos.

'Three million tourists come to Halong Bay every year,' Madam Hu said apologetically. 'Most of them from China. They have little respect for our heritage.

The breathtaking views and geological wizardry of the Bay did not stop Angel from thinking about his upcoming border crossing. The success of an illegal crossing into Laos rested on the word of a psychopath and the owner of a karaoke bar. Angel was not used to relying on others when it came to taking decisions, particularly when his life was at risk. He was the one who calculated the odds, and decided when and how to meet any particular challenge. Ill at ease with the arrangements that had been made he had to trust that the frontiers and border posts were as poorly manned and inefficiently managed as Lai made out.

After dinner that evening Angel went to his room, giving a passing nod to his minder who had settled down for the night in the leather arm chair in the lobby. Angel waited until midnight, and then left the hotel taking the same route as he had done the night before.

Lai was waiting for him. Somewhere in the background a girl was singing '*Staying Alive*', an old Bee Gees hit. An appropriate choice given the occasion. Angel gave Lai $500 and followed him out of the bar to a waiting pickup.

'This is Hoi An, your driver. He speaks good English. You can ask him for anything you might need.'

Angel nodded to Hoi An, and climbed into the pickup.

'Good luck, Mr Angel.'

Dawn light revealed an endless array of hills covered in dense tropical foliage. The road ran parallel to the twisted contours of a river, passing through magnificent stands of giant bamboo. Hoi An, speaking for the first time, said the area was the centre of an illegal trade in wild animals and timber.

'Smugglers bypass the border by cutting their own tracks through the forest or use the river to float the logs downstream into Vietnam. If you follow any of these trails or walk along the river banks you'll see homemade traps made of wood and bicycle brake wire, nearly invisible beneath the leaves.'

'For catching what?'

'Box turtles, snakes, water birds.' Hoi An paused. 'The real money comes from Pangolin.'

'Why Pangolin?'

'Have you been to Ho Chi Minh City?'

'No.'

'Then you've not heard of Thien *Vuong Tuu*. It's a classy restaurant in District 1. Pangolin is on the menu, along with bear, porcupine and bat. If you order pangolin it will cost you $3 a gram. Customers must order it two to three hours in advance and place a deposit based on its weight. When the customer returns for dinner the manager presents the live pangolin to the table, then slices its throat to prove that the meat is fresh and has not been substituted. After dinner they give you the pangolin scales, a popular ingredient in traditional medicines.'

'Are the animals caught locally?'

'No. They are nearly extinct in Vietnam. Most are brought in from Cambodia, Thailand and Laos. The government doesn't allow exotic meat. But the frontiers are so poorly staffed that all sorts of contraband and goods flood into the country.'

'Are you involved?'

'A man has to live. I sell Pangolin for $90 a pound. The basic wage in Vietnam is $36 a month. I can't educate my children on that.'

'I thought schooling was free.'

'That's what they tell you. But it's not. Because schools can't charge fees until the secondary level they ask you to pay for pens, notebooks, uniforms and anything else they can think of. If you don't want your children on the street you have to pay.'

'What about border patrols?'

'If you get caught you pay a small fine. No one gets sent to jail. It's in no one's interest. The police sell the animals they impound back into the black market. Sometimes the big traffickers are taken into custody, but usually they get off. Wildlife crime is not an issue here.'

By the time they finished talking they had drawn up outside the Cau Treo custom's office, a large French colonial building with a colonnade. At one time Cau Treo was an important crossing; now it served only backpackers and local villagers.

Hoi An made good time. They arrived at the border just after six in the morning, an hour before it was due to open. The parking lot besides the building was empty but for a number of distinctive blue and white police cars.

'Is this normal?' Angel asked.

Hoi An shrugged. 'Sometimes the borders guards sleep here overnight rather then drive back to Lak Xao or Vinh. Don't worry. Just shrug if they ask you anything, and give them ten or twenty dollars. Laos is just down the road. Good luck, Mr. Angel.'

Angel got out of the pickup and entered the building. He walked into a large waiting room, sparsely furnished, with a photo of Ho Chi Minh on the wall. As soon as he entered the room two policemen blocked his exit. A third faced him, pointing a pistol at his chest.

'Raise your hands please.'

As he did so one of the officers placed a pair of handcuffs on his wrists. Angel looked at the officer holding the gun. He considered testing himself against the three men, but the six shot revolver was fully loaded and ready to fire.

'You are under arrest.'

'What for?'

'Murder.'

The police had been given their instructions. Protest was pointless. Aquino must have struck shortly after Angel left the hotel. Finding Angel gone, Kai would have given his description to the border police and ordered his arrest. Not for the first time Angel felt himself caught in a bizarre game of make-believe. Only the improbable now seemed to be conjoined with reality. Angel let himself be guided to one of the waiting police cars where he was seated between two armed officers.

8

Contrary to the regulations of the Vietnamese penal code Angel was arrested without court approval and not taken to the Ministry of Interior records office to be fingerprinted. He was taken directly to Prison Camp 5, in Thanh Hóa. For security reasons, so that mail can be sent to prisoners without revealing their whereabouts, camps are known by a code number. Infamous for its harsh and squalid conditions, Camp No. 5 is located in the Hàm Rồng mountains, 150 kilometres south of Hanoi.

The prison was fenced by high walls and watch towers. Angel was led to a detention room through a heavy wooden doorway. Once inside he was ordered to put on a blood stained grey and white uniform bearing the word 'HÌNH SỰ' (criminal) on the jacket. The jacket did not fit over his shoulders and the pants would not fit round his waist. Angel dismissed the offer with a shake of his head. The guards nearest him raised their batons, shouting at him to undress. Seeing that Angel could not be intimidated, and fearful of the outcome if they attacked him, they appealed to the officer who drew out his revolver. For a moment there was a standoff, with no one moving. Then the officer waved his hand dismissively, as if the uniform was of no account, and pointed Angel in the direction of a corridor. On either side of the passageway, illuminated by single bulbs hung on cords, were numbered cells. From the cells came low moans, the subdued cry of pain, or perhaps despair.

Angel was pushed into an airless cell, measuring 5 feet by 5 feet. The cell was too small for him to stand up in or lie down without bending. When the heavy door was slammed shut and the latch fell in place Angel found himself in complete darkness. The only furniture was a bamboo mat encrusted with dirt, and a plastic bucket. The size of the cell did not worry Angel unduly. He had lived through worse. But the darkness was oppressive, almost physical in its saturation.

Angel knew the effects of prolonged darkness from those who had suffered from being in solitary confinement. The absence of sensory stimulation can induce hallucinations and a radical decline in mental functioning. Isolation panic can warp the mind into believing that one is disconnected from reality, creating anxiety attacks that are life threatening Survival when subject to prolonged confinement depends on keeping one's mind active. One must hold on to every sound as if it were a guarantee of life.

Angel was one of 682 prisoners on death row in Vietnam awaiting execution. Executions had fallen behind because firing squads had been replaced by lethal injections which had proved ineffective. The domestic poisons, a cocktail of toxins, far from killing the condemned, left them writhing in agony. Every year a hundred or more prisoners were added to the number awaiting execution. Until the firing squads regrouped, prisoners were confined to cells with no view of the outside world or access to fresh air and natural light. Their only human contact was limited to superficial transactions with prison staff.

The guard's temperament is a key factor in any prison. From a prisoner's perspective the best guards were older men of low rank. A combination of these two conditions more or less ensured an almost decent person. It is even better if they drink.

Such a person is not trying to build a career. The career of a prison guard, and especially of a camp guard, must be lubricated with the blood of prisoners. The guards that Angel had seen were all young men. Notable for their use of truncheon and stick, there would be no help from that quarter.

Angel had not been told how long he would remain in prison. To preserve his health and sanity he set himself a regime of exercise and meditation. By lying diagonally, and regularly changing position, he could ward off the worst effects of cramp and maintain his fitness. His providential disclosure of man's true nature facilitated the acceptance of his condition as a consequence of human activity. The experience of a timeless reality beyond anything that the senses could offer subjected his current state to a conditional event of no lasting consequence.

To explain how and why in extreme moments one may take comfort in the presence of a transcendent truth is beyond our knowing. But like night's shadows that recede before the advancing light, Angel's anxiety was overcome by an assurance that whatever should happen there was an eternal reality in complicity with the human spirit. This does not make light of human suffering, but it robs death of its presumption to have the last word.

If Angel were to die, he would die with one regret: not to have loved and been loved in return. The mutual sympathy, friendship, patriotism and intimacy he shared with his men was never the full swing of one heart to another. A sympathetically awakened feeling of good will is an impulse towards comradeship, but is not a lover's love. The army offered fellowship, but not the love that looks beyond the word 'love' for the substance of its meaning.

Angel's was taken from his cell after just two weeks, less

time than he had anticipated. But Kai had made his point. In the communist world the rule of law, freedom of the individual and so forth, were at the discretion of those in authority. In Vietnam the norms generally recognized in a civilized society were 'subject to cancellation' at any time. Angel had been warned. Failure to cooperate carried penalties.

Angel carried the grime and squalor of his cell. He had lost weight, but his health was intact. The psychological impact of darkness, the nightmare of solitary confinement, was interrupted each morning by a flicker of light as the bowl of rice was pushed through a flap in the cell door. It was sufficient to track the hours, sequence time, and structure the day so as to give it a semblance of normality. The physical experience had been uncomfortable, the darkness oppressive, but overall he had suffered no ill effects.

Angel was led past the 'death' cells to the main prison block. The glare of the overhead bulbs was a painful stab that ran from his eyes to his brain. Stumbling several times over the uneven floor, he was escorted to a row of cells separated by stone walls. Contrary to his hope of being released he was pushed into a cell, only a little bigger than the cells in the isolation block, with five other prisoners. It had no running water, no windows or fresh air. The hygiene bucket was overflowing, its liquid mess spilling onto the stone floor. Pleas to visit the latrine were ignored. Defilement was inevitable. It was a deliberate excremental assault to induce a state of dehumanization.

Angel's cell mates were classified as 'people who committed serious crimes against the people' and had been sentenced to 'long-term education'. But Vietnam's prisons are not re-education camps. They are places of retribution and punishment. The idea that torture, malnutrition, and summary executions encourage loyalty to the State is a fantasy that only a Marxist inspired government could believe.

But for a middle aged German arrested for paedophilia, Angel's cell mates were Vietnamese. Most had been arrested for violating Article 88 of the penal code *'Conducting propaganda against the Socialist Republic of Vietnam,'* one of 29 'crimes' that carried the death penalty. The men had been so severely beaten and broken by hunger and cold that they scarcely acknowledged Angel's presence.

The German, Karl Weiss, was arrested for having sex with an 11 year old girl. He escaped execution because in 2011 the Penal code was amended to exclude the death penalty for child molestation. There are 185,000 prostitutes in Vietnam, and 30% are under the age of 16. His lawyer told the court that because Europeans have difficulty in distinguishing the age of Asian women, Weiss had made an error of judgement and thought the girl was older. The story did not wash because Weiss' name was on the Interpol Paedophile Register. He had come to Vietnam because paedophiles had singled out Hanoi as a 'hot spot' for under age sex and the police easily bribed. Flushed out of Cambodia and Thailand, Vietnam had become the preferred venue for child rape. Sex tourists could download lists of available local children from a web address and 'adopt' them for as long as they were in Vietnam for 5,000 U.S. dollars. Weiss was not serving his full term. He had had his sentence reduced from 25 years to three years by paying the girl's parents $300 for telling the judge that they wanted him released on 'compassionate' grounds.

Vietnam's criminal justice system has only one goal, to punish anyone who goes against the 'Unity of the Party and State'. The word 'Party' stands not just for the CPV, but a whole series of lesser organizations which have little do with implementing the decisions of the National Congress. But since these provincial organs represent the 'aspirations, and mastery of the people' they claim unlimited authority to suppress all 'anti-State tendencies'. Although the constitution guarantees the right of all citizens to 'enjoy freedom of opinion and speech' it is restricted by a host of domestic laws and regulations which prohibit all spoken or written expressions deemed to contravene the interests of the Party. These include "activities aiming to overthrow the people's administration" (Penal Code Article 79, penalty up to death sentence); "undermining national unity policy" (Article 87, penalty up to 15 years in prison); "conducting propaganda against the State of the Socialist Republic of Vietnam" (Article 88, penalty up to 20 years); "disrupting security" (Article 89, penalty up to 15 years); "fleeing abroad or staying abroad to oppose the people's government" (Article 91, penalty up to life sentence). Nor do these draconian penalties end there. Article 92 allows the State to confiscate the property of former prisoners without compensation. Because Party officials are the sole arbitrators of what constitutes a threat, Vietnam has the highest number of political prisoners in Southeast Asia. In the first six months of 2014 there were 83,000 arrests just for subversive language.

Ha Tay, who sat hunched up next to Angel, was sentenced to 25 years for joining a prayer group on the steps of the cathedral in Ho Chi Minh City. His arrest was in contravention of the International Convention on Civil and Political Rights which gives every individual the right to freedom of religious belief. Because religion is contrary to State sponsored atheism, the government turns a blind eye to cadres that seize church property, break up prayer meetings, and generally make life unpleasant for priests and lay persons. Any form of religious worship is a risky business in Vietnam. Because prayer contests the Marxist understanding of religion as the 'opium of the people', an illusory happiness, displaying a reverential attitude in public is cause for suspicion and arrest.

Marx never understood that religion is not a matter of evading reality, but of endeavouring to comprehend reality, an error perpetuated by the CPV.

The other prisoners, with the exception of the German, were serving lengthy sentences for drawing attention to the corruption and land grabbing among members of the provincial people's committees. Their goal terms were harsh because they had voiced their thoughts on the Internet. In a country where all 850 newspapers and magazines and 68 radios stations are run by Party-controlled, military or government agencies, the internet provides the only source of independent news and comment. Since the Party is responsible for guiding public opinion anyone who questions Government policy is likely to find himself behind bars in one of Vietnam's 're-education camps' (a euphemism for indefinite detention borrowed from the Chinese communists).

Angel did not have to look at his cell mates twice to know that after another few months of prison rations he would become just as debilitated. Only the German, who received food parcels from the Embassy was strong enough to stand upright without effort.

Escape was impossible without outside help. Much of Vietnam's interior is composed of rugged mountains and deep valleys covered in dense tropical growth and are sparsely inhabited. Even if Angel was able to leave the camp without detection, his chance of making his way through the jungle to Laos without supplies and a guide were slim. He did not rule out the idea, but his move from the death cells suggested that Kai had something else in store for him.

A week after his transfer to the central prison block, Angel was taken from his cell, told to wash, and given an ill-fitting uniform to replace his soiled clothes. After changing he was escorted to the camp commander's office. Facing Angel was his nemesis, Viet Kai.

'Mr. Angel,' Kai said. 'We meet again.'

'So it seems,' Angel said.

'I regret that our prisons are not up to Western standards. We inherited them from the French who did not build them with their own citizens in mind. On the other hand you appear not to have suffered unduly; but then I expected nothing less.' Kai paused. 'You will be pleased to hear that the criminal who shot Bai Tien has been arrested and executed.'

'You mean Aquino?'

'No. Not Aquino.' Kai smiled. 'A common criminal. We had to act quickly.'

Angel did not have to be told that a quick execution was necessary to silence criticism of Kai's ministry. At any time even prominent members of the Party might find that they had been demoted for no good reason. While Kai was too influential to be dropped from the Politburo, he was nevertheless expected to demonstrate his commitment to the 'overall political mission' of the communist Party. Finding culprits for the assassination of high profile dissidents was one such task.

'Am I free now?'

'Not quite, Mr. Angel. You escaped while under protective custody. You also tried to leave the country illegally. Under

Article 88 of the Penal Code you could be imprisoned indefinitely for either offence.'

Half the prisoners in Camp 5 had been charged under this ordinance. Article 88 does not define what acts are classified as 'violations'. It can be used as a pretext for execution or imprisonment for almost anything.

Kai did not elaborate but said, 'The CPV has many enemies Mr. Angel. It has become necessary to ban political parties, unions and human rights organizations to prevent the spread of anti-socialist propaganda and criticism of the government. Bai Tien belonged to a faction that opposed the government's position on a number of issues. He could not be allowed to continue to undermine the Party's policies.

'I know nothing about his affairs. I never met him, and until you mentioned his name, I had not heard of him.'

Ignoring Angel's comment, Kai continued his denunciation of Tien. 'We live in a communist country, but Bai Tien was not a communist. Tien believed that we should support free enterprise and self-ownership. But it is not State policy to allow private businesses to operate competitively for profit. Unfortunately Mr. Tien did not keep his ideas to himself. We believe he attracted a group of like minded people with the intention of destabilizing the Party.'

Kai took a pamphlet from his pocket and passed it to Angel. 'Read the paragraph I have underlined.'

'Communism is inseparably interwoven with totalitarianism. It prescribes for everyone what they are to think, what they are to believe, and what they may say Police latitude is without limit: they are empowered to take preventive measures against anyone who is merely under suspicion of opposing Party policy If Vietnam is to prosper the government must become more

democratic The economy must become driven by free enterprise with a minimum of government interference and regulations, etc … '

'We believe this was written by Mr. Tien. Sedition carries the death penalty in Vietnam. Fortunately his execution has been carried out for us. Our task is to find Tien's conspirators before they attract more attention.'

Angel thought that he would have liked to have met Bai Tien, but repeated what he had said earlier. 'I've no connection with any person or organization conspiring to undermine the CPV. This is not something I can help you with.'

'On the contrary Mr. Angel, you are one of the few people that can help us.'

'How?'

'By learning the names of Tien's associates.'

Angel shook his head. 'I had not heard of Tien till you mentioned his name. I've no idea who his friends are. Surely with all your resources this is something you would be able to find out. I'm told you have spies everywhere.'

Kai ignored the reference to spies with a dismissive gesture. 'Bai Tien knew many influential people. Some have senior positions in the Secretariat and the Politburo. They are not people we can put under surveillance. We have an idea who they are, but we need more evidence.'

'I can't help you.'

'Give us some credit Mr. Angel. We are not setting you on a wild goose chase. You will be introduced to someone who knows all Tien's affairs – and will not mistake you for one of our "spies".'

'Who is this person?'

'Tien's wife.'

'His wife!'

'Yes.'

Angel laughed. 'Are you suggesting that I seduce Tien's wife, and under cover of intimacy have her disclose the names of her husband's friends?'

'Not "friends" Mr. Angel, but co-conspirators.'

'Without sounding too moralistic, I'm not in the habit of deceiving people's wives. Nor can I think of any reason why she would want to discuss her husband's affairs with me.'

'Mr. Angel,' Kai said, 'you will do as we ask because you do not want to spend the rest of your life in this stinking prison. Nobody knows you are here. To put it bluntly, if you remain here you will die. You've seen the other prisoners.... few of them will ever see the outside again. Many die within a few months of their arrival. Be sensible Mr Angel.'

Kai paused, and then said in a more conciliatory voice, 'What we are asking is not so onerous. Mrs. Tien is what we call a *Viêt Kiều,* a foreign educated Vietnamese. Her close friends are English and American. She is not suspicious of foreigners. I might also add that she is an attractive woman. It is a small service, Mr. Angel, for which the Party will be grateful.'

Angel looked at Kai in a manner that left no doubt as to his feelings. But whatever the ethics of the situation life took priority over death, as Kai knew it would. He also knew that the British embassy would not intervene on Angel's behalf while he had a warrant for Angel's arrest. Embassies in Vietnam are wary of the Ministry of Public Security because it pays no attention to diplomatic immunity.

The Công *an Nhân dân Viêt Nam* was set up in 1977 by the Stasi, the East German secret police. Stasi agents taught Kai's agents how to infiltrate society and develop its oppression of dissidents. False arrests, murder, torture, illegal wire tapping, mail robbery and fraud were all part of its modus operandi. Like the Nazi SS, Kai's Security Branch needed no legal backing for its actions. Its procedures are legitimized by non-official, ideological and political considerations. The Vienna Convention on Diplomatic Relations offers no protection to embassies in Vietnam.

'Mr. Angel, may I take your silence to mean that you agree?'

'You don't give me much choice.'

'Good. You will find a suitcase with your clothes next door. A meal has been prepared for you in the staff dining room. When you are ready a car will take you to your hotel. We will talk again in a few days. In the mean time you are free to come and go as you please.'

'Free?'

'Within limits. Vietnam is one of the 190 members of Interpol. Should you leave the country your description, fingerprints and photos will be sent to law enforcement agencies in all member countries. You will not be able to cross a checkpoint, border post, or frontier where a passport is required without being arrested. But I hope you will not think of leaving us again. You have not yet had time to see our country. There is much beautiful scenery: rugged mountains, sandy beaches, limestone outcrops, and the Mekong and Red River deltas which are biosphere reserves. We welcome Western visitors, Mr Angel. You will find us friendly and obliging. Until next week then.'

9

Angel was given the keys to his old room in the Bao Ninh. The clothes that he had left were hanging in the cupboard and Madam Hu's brochures still lay unopened on the side table. His bed had been made and fresh towels lay out, but otherwise the room was as he had left it.

After several days rest and feeling no ill effects from his confinement, Angel visited one of Hanoi's major attractions, the *Hỏa Lò*, or 'Hell Hole' prison. The decision was not taken because of an interest in prisons, or out of curiosity to compare it with the camp in Thanh Hóa, but because the *Hỏa Lò* was just a block away from the hotel.

Although most of the original prison was demolished in 1996 to make way for Hanoi's first tower blocks, the southernmost corner has been preserved as a museum dedicated to the revolutionaries who died there. The prison was built in 1913 by the French for holding Vietnamese political campaigners. It was part of a network of prisons that included Thanh Hoa (Camp 5). Until the French left Vietnam *Hỏa Lò* was a symbol of colonialist exploitation and the bitterness felt by the Vietnamese towards the French.

Hỏa Lò saw a new lease of life with the arrival of the Americans in 1961. Pilots and crew members shot down during bombing raids over Hanoi and Hai Phong were crowded into single cells. Although Vietnam was a signatory of the Geneva

Convention which holds that prisoners of war merit 'decent and humane treatment', the Vietnamese followed the Soviets by making an exception for those charged with 'crimes against humanity', that is the bombing of Vietnamese towns and cities. The Americans were confined to solitary confinement for long periods and tortured if they refused to broadcast prepared anti-war statements and write letters criticizing U.S. policy and conduct of the war. The torture was such that nearly every American POW made an anti-war statement of some kind during their internment.

There was little difference between the grim cells that held the Americans and those Angel had occupied in *Thanh Hoa.* Both were cramped, airless and dark, and carried the odour of suffering. Other than a display of pre-1954 photographs illustrating the horrors of life in prison during the French colonial period, there was little else to see beyond a sparse collection of rusty shackles, leg irons and a guillotine used by the French to behead Vietnamese revolutionaries.

Thinking of his own arrest, Angel wondered how Kai learned that he had planned to leave the country via the Cau Treo border crossing. The Vietnam-Laos border extends for more than 2000 kilometres. He might easily have chosen one of the other eleven international crossings. It was still a mystery why he had been detained in the first place, or falsely accused of the murder of Bai Tien. Communist double speak made it almost impossible to discover the truth behind any decision or judgement emanating from a government office or official.

As Aquino was the most likely source for answers, Angel retraced his steps to the Golden Goat Bar the evening after his visit to the 'Hell Hole'.

Tam Lai was surprised to see him.

'Mr. Angel! I thought you were in Laos.'

'There was a change of plans.'

'Hoi An said he saw you enter the custom's house. Did anything go wrong?'

Angel dismissed the question with a a non-committal shrug. 'You said that you knew Mr. Aquino.'

'Yes. A big man, as tall as you. He comes here sometimes.'

'Where can I find him?'

'I think he lives in Nha Trang. But I can't be sure.'

'Nha Trang?'

'It's a coastal city,' Lai said. 'It's about eight hundred miles south of here.'

'What else do you know about him?'

'Not much. He comes here to drink. He's not interested in girls.'

'Does Kai ever come here?'

Tam Lai laughed. 'You mean Viet Kai? Not likely. Some of his men maybe. You never know who the police are.'

'What is the best way to Nha Trang?'

'By train. It can take 26 hours. If you take a sleeper it is comfortable enough. Are you planning to find Mr. Aquino?'

'Yes.'

'Did you know that he carries a gun? It is strictly illegal in Vietnam. Even toy guns are prohibited. '

'It does not surprise me.'

'Be careful, Mr Angel. Especially if he has been drinking.'

10

Angel followed Lai's advice and took the train to Nha Trang. Nestled below the bottom lip of the Cai River, Nha Trang has earned its place on Vietnam's tourist mainline because of its wide and beautiful municipal beach. Nha Trang is a city with a population of over 300,000. Finding Aquino would be a matter of luck.

Angel checked into the Tri-Star hotel, a 10 minute walk from the station in the downtown area which swirls around the *Cho Dam* or central market. His first enquiries along the sea front proved abortive. On the second day a waiter in a bar near the bus station told Angel that a man matching Aquino's description dropped in occasionally. He thought the tall *'tây'* (foreigner) lived in Dai Lanh, a small fishing village 80 kilometres north of the city.

Angel rented a car and drove to Dai Lanh along the newly surfaced coast road. Dai Lanh is a patchwork of houses with clay-tile roofs behind a kilometre long beach that curves around Vung Ro Bay. Parking outside an open fronted bar facing the beach Angel asked the owner if he knew of a big foreigner living locally. The man nodded, pointing in the direction of a dirt track that wound its way through a forest of pine trees.

The track was steep, and pitted with corrugations formed by the rain. After a quarter of mile Angel came to a rural farm house with hand-hewn wooden walls and shutter doors. The wood planks for the walls were covered with mud mixed with rice straw and painted white. Under the thatched roof in the front of the house were rows of pillars nicely carved with animals and flowers.

Aquino was waiting for him.

'You have good ears, Mr. Aquino.'

'Not me, Mr. Angel. My dogs. An unexpected surprise. Come inside.' Aquino growled at the two black dogs whose barking had alerted him to Angel's coming. Angel followed Aquino into a room dominated by a large, carved wooden alter adorned with candles and fruit offerings.

'A nice house, Mr. Aquino. Are you a Buddhist?'

Aquino gave a curt shrug in the direction of the alter table. 'That's Hanh's doing. The Vietnamese believe in all kinds of spirits and gods. They think viruses are fallen angels who have been kicked out of heaven.'

'Who is Hanh?'

'She owns this place,' Aquino said, nodding in the direction of the kitchen where Angel and saw a tiny, wrinkled old woman with teeth blackened by a dye made from an aphid-like insect.

Aquino walked to a cupboard and brought out a bottle of *rượu lậu*, a distilled liquor made from glutinous rice. High in alcohol, it was moonshine by any other name.

'What can I do for you Mr. Angel? I thought you were in Laos.'

'Then you didn't know?'

'Know what?'

'The police were waiting for me at Cau Treo.'

'Too bad. I didn't think Kai would be so quick off the mark.'

'How did he know that I had seen Lai?'

'He would have had you followed.'

'The minder was asleep in the lounge.'

'He was a decoy. The real spotter was outside the hotel.'

Angel should have guessed as much. It had been too easy to leave the hotel without being seen.

'Where did they take you?

'To Thanh Hoa, Camp 5.'

'It has a bad reputation. People used to call it camp *Ly Ba So* after the prison head. They say he was a sadistic bastard. How did you get out?'

'Kai.'

'Then he has something in mind for you. Your stay in *Thanh Hoa* was to soften you up.'

'For what?'

'I don't know, but there will be a political twist to it.'

There was, but it was not Aquino's business. 'How long have you been working for Kai?'

'Five or six years.'

'Doing what?'

'I told you Mr, Angel. I get rid of people. Who they are is of no concern. I am given a name and a photograph, and I attend to it.'

'What brought you to Vietnam?' I worked for the Kuratong Baleleng. It was one the leading mafia families in Manila. The mafia was always on the lookout for kids like me who were handy with a knife and a gun and who keep their mouth shut. When they asked if I was interested in doing some 'special work' for them, I said 'for sure'. To test me they had a couple of men drive me to San Juan in down-town Manila. On the way over one of them handed me a short-barrelled .38 with a suppressor on it. When we passed a man on his own walking a dog the driver pulled over and told me to cap him. Without a

~ 65 ~

word I got out of the car, walked up to the man, pointed the gun at the back of his head and shot him. He never even knew he died, or why. When I walked back to the car I could see that the two men were impressed. One of them said, 'I was their man.' When the family wanted a mark to disappear they called me. I've lost count of the men I've killed. But it still gives me a good feeling, like a fix of pure heroin.'

Aquino took another mouthful of *rượu lậu*. It was his third glass, but his voice was steady.

'I kept a cut-down .22 Magnum with a silencer in the car. Sometimes I used two different-calibres on the same target so that it would appear as if there were two shooters. Killing came naturally to me. I have a gift for it. The cops never came close to suspecting that I was responsible for all the bodies they kept finding. There were no witnesses, no clues, no one knew anything.' Aquino paused. 'Taking a life. It means nothing. Did it mean anything to you Mr. Angel? '

'The circumstances were different. It was kill or be killed.'

From the moment Angel joined the army he had adapted himself to obey orders which demanded obedience. Actions which led to the loss of life were morally justified if they served some military objective. It was natural under the circumstances to suspend moral judgements.

'The end is the same, Mr Angel. Someone dies.'

'Yes.'

'I already knew,' Aquino continued, 'when I was quite young, that I would live outside the law. I fantasized about killing people for a long time. I enjoyed my work, the way it made me feel. If anybody fucked with me I could kill him. It made a difference to the way I felt about myself.

'After killing my father I thought about talking to someone.

~ 66 ~

But what would I say to a shrink. "I shot my father when I was twelve, and I should have done it when I was ten. Now I kill people for money, and I like my work." I don't think so.'

Aquino was bipolar, two people in one body, and they were strangers to one another. Sitting alongside Angel, enjoying Angel's company, and talking calmly, no one would take him for a psychopath. But when his thoughts turned to murder, Aquino became a human predator. Aquino may have wished that his life had taken another turn, but he had become accustomed to murder and his ego would not surrender its satisfaction.

'You didn't say what brought you to Vietnam.'

Aquino filled his tumbler with another four fingers of rice alcohol. 'The Philippines are a transit hub for drugs, especially the marijuana grown in the mountainous areas of Northern Luzon and Mindanao. The Kuratong was one of many crime syndicates that set up supply chains in South East Asia. There was plenty of work to go round but the cartels got greedy. They started fighting among themselves. In Caloocan City, part of Metro Manila, there were fifty assassinations in just one week. President Estrada was forced to set up an Anti-Organized Crime Task Force. Panfilo Lacson was told to wipe out the syndicates. In the first month 11 Kuratong were shot dead by the PAOCTF (Presidential Anti-Organized Crime Task Force). The writing was on the wall. It was time to leave. '

'So you came to Vietnam?'

Aquino nodded. 'The Kuratong smuggled marijuana and cocaine into Vietnam through Laos and Cambodia. Their contact in Hanoi was Dinh Tam. Tam was head of a major drug ring that had its centre of operations in Da Nang. Tam and I met a couple of times and I told him where he could reach me. A few months later Kai's narcotics department arrested 32 people, including Tam. Tam had connections in high places and was released. The others were sentenced to death. Tam was let off the hook, but not before giving Kai a list of his contacts. My name was on the list. I was picked up. Kai had nothing on me, but that didn't mean anything. He could have me sent back to Manila, or had me shot, and nobody would be any the wiser. Tam told him I was a contract killer and tight-lipped. Kai offered me immunity in return for carrying out extra judicial killings.

'The VCP make the cartels look like a bunch of 'do gooders'. People in Kai's position can do what they like. Orders and regulations don't apply to them. My first job for Kai was disposing of Tam. I arranged to meet him in Lai's karaoke bar. Disco lights were flashing all round the room. Tam was sitting at a table with a couple of girls. I had a little .38 derringer. When I passed his table I pressed it into the base of his skull. The report of the gun was drowned by the music. An easy kill. I've been working for Kai ever since.'

'And Tien was your last target.'

'Yes. If someone doesn't carry a badge with a red star on his chest he's done away with. You'd be surprised at the people I've taken out. People in very high places.'

'Why you? Why not one of his own people?'

'Kai would like to have his own SS, complete with black cap and a death's-head badge, but this would be too obvious, even for the CPV. They like someone else to do their dirty work. Someone who can keep his mouth shut and won't stir up trouble. Although the Prosecutor's Office has stopped recording shootings by the Security Police the Party wants to show a clean face.'

Aquino had almost finished the bottle of rượu lâu. Angel wondered if Kai knew that his assassin was an alcoholic.

Angel got to his feet. The two black dogs stirred, but fell back after a growl from Aquino.

'Before you leave Mr. Angel, a word of advice. Do whatever Kai wants. If you stand in his way I might get a note with your name on it.'

Thank you for the warning Mr. Aquino.'

11

During the journey back to Hanoi Angel thought about Aquino's parting words. Angel had faced armed men before, but they were visible, or he had foreknowledge of their position. But Aquino would strike when least expected, unseen and unannounced. To get the better of him would depend as much on chance as whose instinct for survival was the sharpest.

The SAS attracted all kinds of men, including those for whom killing human beings was more a sport than a necessary evil. But Aquino was a different case altogether. Unable to break the link between evil and its incarnation in murder, Aquino had become a serial killer. Human life was his to dispense with or not as the case might be. While Angel hoped that he ad seen the last of Aquino he had an uneasy feeling there was unfinished business between them.

Several days after seeing Aquino Angel was back in Kai's office. The black and white photos on the wall behind Kai's desk were a pictorial reminder of the bloody battles that swept through Vietnam from Haiphong to Saigon. Photos of patrols through muddy fields, the pockmarked walls of a Buddhist temple, a Viet Cong camp against a landscape of severed trees and blasted earth called to mind his own days of warfare.

'Most of these photos,' Kai said, noticing Angel's interest, 'were taken on the Ho Chi Minh trail. It ran a thousand miles, all the way through Southern Laos and North-eastern Cambodia to the highlands of South Vietnam. It is an area of rugged mountains, triple-canopy jungle and dense rainforests. Trucks could drive the entire length of the trail without emerging from the canopy except to ford streams or cross them on crude bridges built beneath the water's surface. The Americans tried to disrupt the supply routes by dumping powdered soap in palletized bags over the trail. It was supposed to keep the mud holes from drying up and to cause landslides. It was a failure. Our road crews quickly overcame the problem by laying bamboo matting on the soaped areas. Another ineffective scheme, which cost the American tax payer $3 million a year, tried to extend the monsoon season and flood the trail by seeding clouds with chemicals. It was the first large scale effort to manipulate the weather for military purposes. If it increased the rainfall it had no effect.

Kai opened a drawer and drew out a faded pamphlet which he passed to Angel.

'I keep this as a reminder of my time on the trail. The Americans dropped millions of theses pamphlets to discourage our troops.'

The pamphlet depicted the skull of a North Vietnamese soldier. Beneath the picture was the text:

WAS THIS YOUR SON, HUSBAND, BROTHER, COMRADE?

This one of the more than 2000 Northern soldiers who died at Plei Me in November 1965. Many thousands have died in other battles and many thousands will continue to die if they don't come over to the South Vietnamese or allied forces. Only these will live to return home'

'We used these propaganda leafless for lighting fires and other purposes which you may guess. Today,' Kai continued, 'a large section of the trail, a web of tracks, roads and waterways, has been reclaimed by tropical growth. But the main artery, many thousands of miles long, has been transformed into the Ho Chi Minh National Highway. It is our largest public works project since the end of the war. It took a North Vietnamese soldier six months to make the trek from Hanoi to Ho Chi Minh City. Today you drive along the same route at 60 mph.

Kai was silent for a minute. 'Those who have not lived through the war will never know what it was really like. What the visitor does not see, and what words cannot tell, is the sweat, the sickness, and the death that accompanied each step of the way. Thousands of North Vietnamese men and women gave their lives to maintain the trail and carry supplies and munitions to our forces in the South. Now it has become a tourist attraction. You may liked to see it.'

'Perhaps one day,' Angel said, 'As you know I have had little time for sightseeing. My excursions to date, other than those taken with Madam Hue, have got no further than the Hoa Lo Prison Museum.'

'Hoa Lo is a legacy from the French. Even during the Second World War when Indochina was occupied by the Japanese the French continued to use Hoa Lo for political prisoner agitating for independence.'

Kai paused. 'After the Japanese surrender Ho Chi Minh declared Vietnam independent under a Viet Minh government. If the French had recognized Vietnam's right to independence we would have been saved further years of war. Instead they established an infantry base in Dien Bien Phu close to the border with Laos to prevent our further occupation of the region. France's only hope of avoiding military defeat was to appeal to the United States. What was a local war between us and the French escalated into an American war lasting more than nineteen years.

'I was only a boy when the French were defeated at Den Bien Phu. But my father lived under French rule for most of his life. The French called their occupation of Vietnam *mission civilisatrice*. They chose not to see that we had a history even older than their own. The French thought that no greater honour could befall a people than for them to absorb their culture.

'A small number of students were given scholarships to study in France. Most, however, had to suffer an education system aimed at breaking our identity. The French reinforced their way of life by stressing the supremacy of all things French – their language, arts, beliefs, customs, institutions, laws. Local temples, monuments and houses, some of which had stood for a thousand years, were destroyed. The Vietnamese names of cities, towns and streets were changed to French names. It was cultural genocide.

'Forget *mission civilisatrice*. The French had only one purpose in mind: to exploit Vietnam for France's benefit. French companies transformed Vietnam's subsistence economy into a proto-capitalist system, based on land ownership and low wages. They seized vast swathes of land and reorganised them into large plantations. Where there were labour shortfalls, Viet farmers were brought in from outlying villages: sometimes conscripted at gun point, and were treated like slaves. In the 20 years between the two world wars, one Michelin-owned rubber plantation recorded 17,000 deaths from malnutrition and disease.

'During the 1920s and 1930s when other colonial administrations in Southeast Asia reduced the scope of their opium monopolies, French intelligence and paramilitary agencies took over the opium traffic in order to finance their covert operations. As soon as the civil administration abolished some aspect of the trade, French intelligence services proceeded to take it over, purchasing raw opium from the Hmong hill-tribes in central and northern Vietnam. Opium smoking dens, cosmetically renamed "detoxification clinics," sold unlimited quantities of opium. By the 1930s Vietnam was producing more than 80 tonnes of opium a year. Before the French established an opium franchise only the Chinese residents smoked opium, and in such small quantities that it was not worth refining locally. To encourage consumption the French built an efficient opium refinery in Saigon to process raw Indian resin into prepared smoker's opium. The new factory devised a special mixture of opium that burned quickly, encouraging the smoker to consume more opium than he might ordinarily.

'The social costs of opium addiction were heavy. Large numbers of plantation workers, miners, and urban labourers spent their entire salaries in Government dens. Vietnamese addiction soon rose so sharply that it accounted for one third of the colonial administration's income. By 1935 France's collective sales of rice wine, salt and opium were earning more than 600 million francs per annum (the equivalent of $US5 billion today).

'Ho Chi Minh said that it was this exploitation that turned him into a nationalist. He dedicated his life to a political program that would draw all Vietnamese into a struggle for independence.'

Kai paused. 'Forgive me Mr. Angel, I did not ask you here to talk history. But for us the war against the French and Americans was a matter of life or death. For the French and the

Americans it was simply an unhappy chapter in their history. It was not the same for us.

'Now let us return to the subject of Mrs. Tien. You agreed to assist us in learning the names of her husband's associates. We share a common interest in bringing this business to a close.'

Angel smiled at the use of the word 'we', but did not comment.

'I understand your reservations,' Kai said, but I am asking no more than your own security service might ask. You will understand that it is sometimes necessary to sacrifice one's values in favour of maintaining national security.'

'When and where am I to have the pleasure of meeting Mrs. Tien?'

'The American Ambassador has a garden party on the last Friday of every month. Mrs. Tien will be there, and so will I. You will come as my guest.'

12

The Ambassador's party was at the Ambassador's Residence, not the embassy, which was overcrowded and lacked a reception room. Unlike the embassy, a nondescript building protected by a high wall in Lang Ha street, the Residence is a fine example of 20th century Colonial architecture. After the French left Hanoi the building was included in an exchange of property between the United States and Vietnam. Its first resident after the exchange was Ted Osius, the first openly gay American ambassador in East Asia.

Angel met Kai outside the Residence as agreed. Because Diplomacy being high on his list of priorities for an ambassador, the guests were mostly local and expat business men, staff from other embassies and aid agencies, and Chiefs of Sections. After introducing Angel to the Ambassador, Kai led Angel across the room towards a woman wearing an *ao dai,* the traditional Vietnamese full-length, figure-hugging split tunic. Angel was immediately taken by her beauty. The woman was Mrs. Tien.

'Mrs. Tien, permit me to introduce Mr. Angel. Mr. Angel is helping us with our security arrangements.'

Angel smiled, and shook hands. Her hand was small, soft, delicate, and disappeared into Angel's as their hands met. After the introduction, Kai excused himself and left to speak to an acquaintance on the far side of the room.

For two people who preferred to listen than talk, it surprised Angel and Mrs. Tien how easily they fell into conversation with each other. When Kai was out of earshot, Mrs. Tien asked Angel about his association with the Security Chief. Angel said that Kai was his contact with the Ministry, but otherwise he had little to do with him, that is expertise was not police work but counter-terrorism.

When it came time to leave Mrs. Tien asked Angel if they could meet the following day. Angel guessed from the seriousness with which the request was uttered that it was not an invitation to get better acquainted, thought he hoped this was part of it, but an appeal for help and advice. Angel agreed at once.

When they said good-bye their hands touched again. The feel of her skin awakened a quickening pleasure. It was a new sensation for Angel.

Next morning Angel received a phone call from Kai. 'How did you and Mrs. Tien get on?'

'Well enough.' For some reason he resented the question, as if Kai was treading on something personal and private.

'So you will be seeing each other again?'

'We have agreed to meet to meet at the Sheraton for lunch.'

'Good,' Kai said. 'Take your time. These things cannot be rushed. In the mean time I will arrange for Madam Hu to show you more of our city.'

'No thank you,' Angel said firmly. 'I prefer to find my own way round.'

Kai's offer, made without preconditions, was the first thaw in a relationship which at best could be called civil. Kai did not need Madam Hu or Luong Van to keep tabs on Angel. More than six million Vietnamese belong to the country's state security and police, roughly one-sixth of its 43-million working population. The streets were alive with Kai's men. Kai could track Angel's every foot step if he chose to. As it was Angel had no intention of skipping the country. For the first time since arriving in Vietnam he felt that his luck had changed.

13

Angel arrived at the Sheraton ahead of Mrs. Tien so that he could choose a table overlooking Hoan Kiem Lake. Mrs. Tien arrived looking even lovelier than Angel remembered. After shaking hands, feeling again her gentle warmth, Angel suggested they call each other by their Christian names. She told him that her English friends called her 'Nan' because they found her Vietnamese name, Nguye^t, too difficult to pronounce. Angel said his Christian name was Michael which she translated as *'phát âm'*, but said she preferred to call him by his English name.

'Mr. Kai said that you were helping him with his security arrangements.'

'It's a broad description. It covers everything from counter-insurgency and terrorism to quite ordinary surveillance. Why do you ask?'

'I'm being blackmailed.'

She told Angel that a man had called demanding a million US dollars to protect her warehouse from an arson attack. The building was particularly vulnerable because it held a large export order due to be dispatched at the end of the week.

'You should talk to Kai.'

'Kai?' She shook her head. 'For all I know he might be behind it. The man who made the call was speaking for someone else, someone with enough influence to know that he would not be incriminated. Arson attracts the death penalty in Vietnam. Whoever is behind this must have the police or a government minister in his pocket.'

'What else did he say?'

'He knew about our garment factory in Hai Ba Tung. He said it would also be set on fire if I didn't pay up.'

'Could it be one of your employees?'

'No' She shook her head. 'My husband looked after our people very well. I trust their loyalty. They would not go behind his back.'

'I still think you should talk to Kai, or let me talk to him for you. His way of doing things might be questionable, but he has the resources to find out who is behind this.'

'You have much to learn about Vietnam. The big gang bosses work hand in hand with the communists. I am not talking about rank and file members, but senior politicians, members of the Central Committee and even the Politburo. One of Kai's top men, the Vice-minister for police, Bui Quoc Huy, was expelled from the Central Committee, but only after a huge public outcry for his defence of Nam Cam. I don't trust any of them. Not even Kai.'

'Who was Nam Cam?'

'A crime boss. He built up a vast criminal enterprise in Ho Chi Minh City. It included a string of gambling dens, cockfighting rings, drug dealing, and restaurants that fronted for brothels. Hundreds of people, including police, government officials and journalists were in his pocket. Cam's influence with the police in Ho Chi Minh City was so extensive that police from other provinces had to be sent in to arrest him.'

'So he was arrested?'

'Yes, eventually. Kai had no option. Cam's influence

threatened the credibility of the Party and the police. The crackdown following Cam's arrest resulted in the arrests of dozens of police officers, several high-ranking prosecutors, and two members of the central committee of Vietnam's Communist Party. Nam Can was found guilty of murder and bribery and sentenced to death by firing squad. In spite of the evidence against him he was defended to the last by Quoc Huy, Kai's Vice-minister for police. When the full extent Huy's relationship with Cam became known he was expelled from the Central Committee.'

'That's all?'

'No. He was demoted from lieutenant general to major general. Had it been anybody else, he would have been shot.'

'Are you sure that Kai knew about Quoc Huy's dealing with Cam?'

'Yes. Everyone knew that Huy was in Cam's pocket. Another thing, Kai had Huy arrested just before the Central Committee convened to discuss leadership changes ahead of the opening session of the National Assembly. Kai knew that if he hushed up the truth about his Vice Minister's dealing with Cam it would reflect badly on himself. He might even have had to stand down.'

Surprised by Kai's role in the affair, Angel returned to the subject to the threatened arson attack. 'Are there local security firms that offer round the clock protection?'

'There are one or two in Hanoi. But because it is illegal to carry a weapon in Vietnam their role is limited. Several provincial police operate a security service on the side. But they are not to be trusted.'

'When is the money due?'

'In two days time.'

'How is it to be paid?'

'To a numbered bank account in Panama.'

'In this case he must have an anonymous company in Panama with local directors. His name would not be registered, and the money almost impossible to trace. Can you take me to the warehouse?'

'Yes. What is it that you want to see?'

'For the moment, just the layout.'

The warehouse was a large double story building in an industrial site on the outskirts of Hanoi. The entrance was by way of a sliding corrugated iron door wide enough to accommodate a lorry. Inside the warehouse a dozen men were busy on forklift trucks, stacking and moving bales of cloth. Angel was quick to see that if the bales were strategically placed the building and its contents could be readily protected.

Angel told Nan that the warehouse could be made safe, but that he would need Kai's cooperation. Although not wanting to be in Kai's debt, she reluctantly agreed. Angel gave the foreman a diagram showing where the bales of cloth were to be stacked. Anyone caught between the row of bales would be at the mercy of those hidden above them.

14

There had been a subtle change in Kai's relationship with Angel since his release from prison. Angel's tacit acceptance of his detention, self-possession and assurance had gained Kai's respect. Moreover they shared a similar background and experienced many hardships in common. Both men had faced enemy fire, faced death, and experienced fear. It is the privilege of such experiences to bring men together.

Seated in Kai's office, Angel came straight to the point. 'Mrs. Tien is being blackmailed. If she doesn't pay up her warehouse will set on fire.'

'Threats of this kind are rare in Vietnam. They can usually be traced to criminals who have the backing of corrupt police or politicians. Did she contact the police?'

'No. She has little confidence in them.'

'She could have come to me'.

'She remembers the incident with Quoc Huy.'

'That was unfortunate. Huy was in Ho Chi Minh City, 900 miles from Hanoi. As soon as I heard about his dealings with Cam he was suspended. But we are not here to discuss Huy.'

Angel nodded. 'My guess is the blackmailer wants to take over her business. It would not be difficult for someone in the same line of work to learn that she has an export order ready for shipment. If blackmail is rare, then it is likely the blackmailer has the protection of the police or someone in government.'

'Our legal framework for tackling corruption is not well developed. The privatisation of state-owned companies has provided the opportunity for people to appoint themselves and their families as executives, creating a class of wealthy businessmen, many with close government connections.'

Angel knew from Nan that corruption continues to negatively influence Vietnam's business environment. Companies are likely to experience bribery, political interference and facilitation payments. In spite of on-going reforms, Vietnam is one of the world's most corrupt countries, and corruption has never been more excessive than under current leadership. For every $10 assigned to any public project, $7 goes into somebody's pocket. In other words 70% of Vietnam's state budget is being stolen.

'We have taken a number of steps to address corruption,' Kai said. 'I acknowledge that these efforts have not brought about expected results, due mainly to a large implementation gap and lack of enforcement. On the other hand we will not hesitate to prosecute corrupt officials. Last year four executives from former state-owned companies were sentenced to death for bribery and fraud; two others were sentenced to life in prison. More recently the Hanoi People's Court sentenced Pham Thanh Tan, the former general director of the State-owned Bank for Agriculture and Rural Development to 22 years in prison for corruption.'

One of the steps mentioned by Kai was the decision to put the CSCAC (the Central Steering Committee for Anti-Corruption) under the Politburo. It is painfully obvious that the Party will resist punishing its own corrupt members, especially when these segments form the upper hierarchy of the Party. Angel might have told Kai that as long as the criminal code prohibits speech that is critical of the government, the inability of media and non-governmental organizations to hold government officials to account will only add to corruption despite all efforts to prevent it.

But Angel had not come to talk to Kai about ethics and corruption, but arson and blackmail.

'Time is not on our side. I want to call the man's bluff. Let the deadline pass, and then hit him when he tries to torch the building. I've had the stock arranged so that there is a 'kill zone'. Anyone entering the warehouse will be trapped between rows of bales. I need three or four men, armed with semi-automatic carbines and a AK-47 for myself. Your men will have a clean shot before drawing fire. The blackmailer will not be among those sent to burn the building, but the shock of being met with so much firepower will curb his appetite for further adventures of this kind.'

'We will do as you say Mr. Angel.' Than smiling, Kai said, 'In spite of your reservations regarding our methods, you can see that there are advantages of acting without regard to existing legislation.'

'I'm all for taking decision without them having to be first approved by some hierarchy of officials and bureaucrats. Very rarely do they have the detailed knowledge of the man on the spot. My concern is the persecution of those who question government policies and expose corruption. Than Hoa is full of people who have been arrested for such vague offences as "conducting propaganda" or "subversion of the people's administration".'

'Mr. Angel we still live under Ho Chi Minh's shadow. We are the beneficiaries of his Marxism-Leninist polices. Whether these are 'right' or not only history will tell. In the mean time we are obliged act against individual members of the public whose views are not in accord with Party policy.'

'Did Ho advocate indoctrination and propaganda, secret police, prisons and torture?'

'Ho's Marxism came through reading Stalin and Mao. Perhaps we interpret his ideas too forcefully at times. But the interests of the Party must prevail against the interest of individuals.'

'There maybe arguments that concentration camps and torture make for a safer country, there are no arguments that they make for a better country.'

15

Nan followed Angel's instructions and did not comply with the blackmailer's demands. Several days after the deadline five masked men broke into the warehouse. Two men carried Thompson submachine guns; the preferred weapon of South Vietnamese troops during the Vietnam War, the others carried US army jerry cans of petrol.

Angel threw the light switch as soon as the men broke into the building. Taken by surprise the two armed men started firing blindly and were brought down by Kai's men. The others made a dash for the open door and ran into Angel holding an AK-47.

The living and the dead were bundled into a police van which had been concealed behind the warehouse. The whole operation had lasted no more than a few minutes.

The following morning Angel called Nan and told her that the arsonists had been arrested. The blackmailer had not been identified, but the survivors were being questioned and Kai was hopeful of getting a name. The two leading communist newspapers, the Nhan *Dan* and the *Sai Gon Giai Phong*, ran headlines praising the People's Public Security for their zeal in combating crime and the bravery of its officers.

After Angel gave Kai an account of the night's proceedings, Kai admitted that that violent crime is becoming a serious problem due to rising unemployment, particularly in the northern ports of Halong City and Haiphong.

'Poverty is the deepest root of crime in Vietnam. Even with a decade of impressive economic growth and poverty reduction, Vietnam remains a low-income country. The current salary level for public servants only meets 50-60 percent of their living standards, a sum that is neither enough to regenerate working capacity nor reflect the real value of their labour. When officials cannot match what they perceive as their daily needs through their salaries, some adopt or are forced to adopt corrupt practises.

'After the Japanese surrendered we thought we could apply Ho's Marxist vision of a new economic order which would ensure that our needs are met equitably. But de Gaulle would not accept a unified Vietnam under Communist rule. To make the point he sent 80,000 French troops into the southern half of Vietnam laying claim to France's previously occupied territory. The French taught us about liberty, equality and fraternity, and then said that these ideas were for Frenchmen only. We are an educated people. We could have formed the nucleus of a Vietnamese administration capable of making a smooth transition from colonial to a post-colonial government. But the French could not bring themselves to think of the Vietnamese as equals.

'Anyone caught reading Ho's pamphlets were shot, beheaded, or had his arms cut off. Thousands of piastres were offered to anyone who brought in a revolutionary cadre's head. Families whose members had secretly joined the communists were arrested, their houses burnt, their property confiscated. Refusing to negotiate with the Viet Minh, Ho withdrew the Viet Minh army from the cities and launched a guerrilla war. Ho's words at the start of the campaign were prophetic: *If they force us into war, we will fight The struggle will be atrocious, but the*

Vietnamese people will suffer anything rather than renounce their freedom.'

'The fighting lasted 13 years, till May, 1954 when we overran the French at Dien Bien Phu. Confident that the Viet Minh could not possibly transport sufficient heavy artillery through the rough mountain terrain, the French generals ignored the warnings of their own artillery specialists. When the artillery duel began in March 1954, the French were shocked to find themselves outgunned. The Viet Minh had two hundred heavy artillery pieces, hauled by eighty thousand Viet Ming porters across the mountains, to the French garrison's twenty-eight heavy guns. Within a month the Viet Minh had silenced the French counter batteries and overwhelmed their garrison.

'Twenty-four hours later, on May 8, 1954, an armistice (the Geneva Accords) brought the war an end, and 75 years of French colonialism. The war had cost nearly a million lives – for what? To satisfy de Gaulle's ego, and absolute faith in the grandeur of France?

'The Americans saw the defeat of the French as a setback in its efforts to resist the spread of communism. President Kennedy, on the pretext that returning Viet soldiers to their homes in the south posed a threat to the regime in the South, provided money, arms, and military advisors to the ARVN (Army of the republic of South Vietnam). All the signs pointed to an even more deadly war. Only this time the 'imperialist' power was the United States.

'My father was badly wounded at Dien Bien Phu and died the following year. I joined the Viet Cong that same year. I had learned a lot about guerrilla warfare from my father and from reading Ho's books. When I met Ho four years later he asked me to join him in training the Viet Cong in preparation for a guerrilla war against the south.

'My first contact with the Americans was in 1963. By then there were already 15,000 U.S. military in South Vietnam. We had no Skyhawks, Chinooks, or B52s. Our war was on the ground. We avoided the set piece battles that the Americans favoured: great waves of helicopters and massive air support. We steered clear of jungle tracks and clearings, running patrols through bamboo thickets and almost impenetrable jungle. Thick overhead foliage filtered out almost all the sunlight, making it difficult to see. Matted vines held the heat. It was like moving through an airless oven. In places the growth was so thick that we had to pull the vines apart with our hands.

'Contrary to all the rules of engagement the Americans bombed our villages irrespective of civilian deaths. My own hamlet, Tu Cung, was a casualty. Jet aircraft spewed jellied fire over the village. The villagers thought that it was falling from heaven. Flames leapt through the air across treetops, exploding in patches along an area fifty yards wide by three-quarters of a mile long. Napalm. My uncle said the ground was writhing in flames. One canister fell on the temple, destroying everything near it, including our house. When the smoke cleared, my uncle found the charred remains of my mother, her sister, her husband and their two children.'

All Angel could do was to express sympathetically, with gestures that accompany such stories, that one is faced with something incomprehensible.

Kai took a copy of 'Life' magazine dated December 1973 from the bookshelf and passed it to Angel. The cover page was titled 'The Year in Pictures'. It had only one item related to the Vietnam War. It was a two-page spread of a portrait of a smiling nine-year-old girl at home in Trang Bang, inset with the picture of her running naked, her body scorched raw from a napalm strike by a South Vietnamese Skyraider. The picture of the terrified girl appeared on the front pages of newspapers all over the world and remains one of the most indelible images of the Vietnam War. The caption under the Life portrait read: *Nan Phuc, Memories Masked by A Smile.*

'I assure you, Mr. Angel, that even after all these years, there are many of us whose memories are still masked by a smile.

'Our war with the Americans lasted 19 years. It was an interregnum of violence unparalleled in our history. The Americans viewed the war as a tactical exercise whose outcome would be determined by controlling territory and winning battles. But for the Vietnamese it was a continuation of the drive for independence initiated against the French. You may have seen Ho's message in the War Museum to the Vietnamese people: "Nothing is as dear to the heart of the Vietnamese as independence and liberation." It became our motto.

'The real tragedy,' Mr. Angel, 'is that given a few more months, and there would never have been a war. Ngo Dinh Diem and Hi Ch Ming were on the very of a political settlement. It called for the end of military assistance to the Diem government, withdrawal of all U.S. forces, and the formation of a coalition government in the South leading in to the eventual unification of Vietnam.

'Kennedy could not accept a neutral Vietnam. "I can't let Vietnam go the communists," he said "and then go and ask these people" – the voters of America – "to re-elect me. We've already given up Laos to the communist, and if I give up Vietnam I won't be able to go to the people."

To avoid Vietnam becoming a neutral county Kennedy put his re-election ahead of the lives of his soldiers and those of the Vietnamese. He authorised the CIA to support a military coup led by General Van Minh to have Diem killed. Diem was arrested and bundled into an armoured personnel carrier where he was shot. Kennedy's assassination, which occurred three weeks later, was exhaustively investigated by official commissions. But neither the American nor South Vietnamese government ever conducted a public enquiry into Diem's death.

'Much to the dismay of the Americans, General Minh and his colleagues were even less capable than Diem of creating a stable government that could defeat the Viet Cong. The U.S. had either to admit defeat and allow Vietnam to fall to the communist or increase its military involvement. Lyndon Johnson, Kennedy's successor, chose the latter, believing what all of the men surrounding Kennedy believed - that fighting the communists was essential to America's national security. It was a decision now seen as one of America's most tragic foreign policy entanglements.

'After the war Vietnam was in a state of physical ruin. The economy was in chaos. Vietnam, a country full of paddy fields, had to import rice. In peace talks the US agreed to pay $3.5bn in reconstruction aid to mend our shattered infrastructure. But the money was never forthcoming. In fact they demanded that Hanoi repay the millions of dollars borrowed by its enemy, the old Saigon.

'Worse was to come. The United States imposed a trade embargo, cutting off Vietnam's war-wrecked economy from US exports and imports and also those from other countries. It put pressure on the IMF, the World Bank and UNESCO to deny Vietnam aid. The Americans conceded that Agent Orange caused serious illness and birth defects and paid $2bn compensation - to its own veterans. Vietnamese victims, more than 2 million of them, got nothing.

'When Ho Chi Minh died in 1969, four years before the last U.S. troops left Vietnam, we pledged to carry on the struggle. His mantle fell on those like myself who had been fighting against Westerners for most of their adult lives. Victory was not achieved without loss. Our combat deaths were 12 times more than that of the Americans.'

Kai was silent. 'The dead are numbers, the wounded can be counted. But there is no arithmetic for suffering. War is the scarlet thread that runs through our history.'

Another pause. 'I tell you these things,' Mr. Angel, 'because I would like you to have a favourable impression of the communist party. If you understand our past you will have a better appreciation of our policies and the challenges that face us.

'Our legal procedures and bureaucratic practices are largely Soviet inspired. But we are now in a state of transition. The hard line ideologues that fear the effect of a free market system are in the minority. Democratic ideals are taking root in Vietnamese society and challenging the CPV's monopoly on power. We have already taken the first steps toward political liberalization. But it will take time for these changes to work through the system.

'It is unfortunate that you were subject to some irregularities on your arrival, but I trust we can make amends for these. I regret that events, which I now regard as circumstantial, caused you some distress. I suggest Mr. Angel, that we put the past behind us.'

It was the closest Angel ever got to learning about the 'irregularities' that led him to Prison Camp 5 in Thanh Hóa.

16

In the days that followed Angel and Nan met regularly at Gia Ngu, a restaurant on *Ho Hoan Kiem Lake* (Lake of the Restored Sword). While the lake is small, one can walk round it in thirty minutes, and is not known for its beauty, it is the soul of the city for those who live in Hanoi. The lake takes its name from the Vietnamese emperor, Le Loi, who led a successful uprising against the Chinese in the 15th century. While fishing he netted a magic sword which gave him superhuman powers. After defeating the Chinese he made his capital in Hanoi, calling the city *Dong Kinh* (Tonkin). While preparing a sacrifice to thank the spirit of the lake the miraculous sword flew from its scabbard into the mouth of a golden turtle. Restored to the gods, legend has it that the sword will reappear when the country is under threat.

Strangers might imagine that Nan, slim and petite, and the big Englishman with the blue eyes and confident smile, had little in common. But it was not so. Both had lived unconventional lives. Nan fled from Saigon as part of the diaspora when she was still a girl, leaving home for another life in another country. Angel's life had been one of conflict and constant travelling from one hotspot to another. Neither had known the more intimate aspects of love. Nan's marriage to Tien was without sexual significance. And Angel's encounters with women had been casual and fleeting.

It was April, Nan's preferred month in Hanoi. After one late lunch they walked along the lake's edge. The afternoon light unrolled in streams, giving the water an almost magical quality. Nature was caught in a spell of quiet and tense glory, unwilling to fade. When they reached the Ngoc Son Temple, Nan took Angel's hand. That gesture, so ordinary in itself, brought to consciousness what they felt for each other. At that moment they knew, if they were not yet in love, the time would not be long in coming.

These pleasurable days, such as Angel had rarely experienced, were interrupted by a call from Aquino.

'Angel?'

'Yes.'

'It's Aquino. I'll meet you tonight in Lai's bar. Be there.' No reason, no explanation.

Annoyed by Aquino's presumption Angel was tempted to decline, but then thought better of it. Aquino sat by himself, a half empty bottle of Mekong Whisky at his elbow. As soon as Angel sat down, Aquino faced him and said, almost accusingly, 'Kai has to go.'

Taken aback, Angel looked at Aquino, waiting for him to continue.

'I've got enough on Kai to bring down the whole bloody Politburo.'

Aquino poured himself another glass of whisky. 'I read about the shootout in the warehouse. I knew you were behind it. It's not the Vietnamese way of doing things. It was too well planned. Kai would have had the whole army surround the building.'

Aquino had been drinking and was jumping from one subject to another.

'I can't get to Kai. When he wants a job done he uses a messaging service.' Aquino paused. 'Do you have a gun?'

'No.'

Aquino put a small pistol on the table and pushed it towards Angel. It was the .38 derringer.

'It will fit in the palm of your hand. Get close. Kill with the first shot. The recoil makes it hard to control the second.'

Had it been anyone but Aquino, Angel would have told the man he was drunk and to put the gun away.

'Why Kai? Why now?'

'I'm a threat. I know too much. '

'It's not that easy,' Angel said, relaxing his voice. 'I only see Kai when he wants to see me. To get to his office I have to go through security and pass through a metal detector. And that's not the end of it. One of his men is stationed permanently outside his door. Anyone entering is searched. I've no love for Kai, but forget about getting to him in his office.'

Aquino looked at Angel without expression. Finally he reached across the table and put the derringer back in his pocket.

'I thought as much, but I needed to make sure. There are other ways.'

'Such as?'

'During a demonstration. Kai wants you to think that he has everything under control: no strikes, no protests, and no riots. It's not the case. People are protesting every day about corruption, embezzlement, and the illegal sale of state land. The peasants have no voice. If they complain they risk arrest and imprisonment. Do you read the papers? Earlier this week thousands of villagers in Thai Binh protested against rice prices and compulsory contributions to infrastructure projects. Yesterday In Son La hundreds of people were arrested for staging a protest against the relocation of their villages to make way for a power station.'

'What has this to do with Kai?'

'There will be a demonstration in Hanoi next week. The government has put a compulsory purchase order on 200 hectares of land for an industrial park. The families involved have refused compensation because the land was valued at only a fifth of its actual value. There is no private property in Vietnam. People only receive the right to use land, not to own it. The law allows the government to revoke these rights whenever they want. With no legal redress, the evicted families have called for a show of strength against the government. Thousands of people will turn up.

'Kai is responsible for public order. He knows that riots are contagious. Those in power hate them and fear them: they are unpredictable. Kai's failure to crack down on riots in Đà Lạt and elsewhere reflects badly on his authority. He cannot let the police be pushed back in Hanoi.'

'And you think he will direct operations himself?' Angel did not hide the scepticism in his voice. 'Kai will delegate the responsibility to his subordinates.'

Aquino grunted. Sober he might have realised that both schemes were madcap ideas. Whatever the reason for Aquino's sudden vendetta against Kai, it was not something that Angel wanted to become involved in. Angel was sure that Kai had forbidden Aquino to leave Vietnam. Nor would Kai be troubled by Aquino's list of 'judicial killings'. The merest whiff of blackmail on Aquino's part would see him arrested and shot.

Angel kept his patience, sympathetic to Aquino's concerns, not wanting Aquino to think that Kai found Angel the more reliable solution to the Party's problems

'Forget Kai. You're the least of his worries.'

Angel got to his feet. 'Good bye, Aquino.'

Aquino did not look up.

17

When Nan asked Angel to accompany her to St. Joseph's to celebrate the feast of St. Jean-Théophane Vénard, he agreed, not out of veneration for the saint, or for the opportunity to worship, but to please her. Angel was not irreligious, but being unused to prayer, he found worship no more than lip repetition, far removed from the silence called for by his own understanding of God.

St. Joseph's is situated west of Hoan Kiem Lake in the old Quarter. Although it serves as the cathedral for the Roman Catholic Archdiocese of Vietnam it is unlikely that Angel would have noted its existence. Badly weathered and in need of restoration it is omitted from most guide books.

Built in 1886 by French missionaries on the site of an ancient Buddhist temple, the high vaulted interior is painted red and yellow (red signifying love and fertility, and yellow, wealth and prosperity) in accord with Vietnamese concerns. The tall stained glass windows were made in France and miraculously made it to Vietnam without damage.

Théophane Vénard was ordained as a priest in 1852, and a year later made his way to Northern Vietnam. His arrival coincided with an edict by the anti-Christian emperor Minh Mang forbidding Christians to practise their faith. Vénard continued to exercise his ministry at night, and then more boldly during the day which led to his capture and beheading.

His head, after being impaled at the top of a pole, was removed by Christians and hidden until it was safe to expose. His remains rest in the crypt at the *Missions Estrangers* in Paris.

Théophane was one of 300,000 Vietnamese martyrs recognized by the Vatican. The sum is made up of those persecuted during the missionary era of the 17th century, killed in the politically inspired persecutions of the 19th century, and martyred during the Communist purges of the 20th century. According to the Vatican the pain suffered by these Vietnamese saints is the worst in the history of Christian martyrdom. Branded on the face with the words *"ta dao"* (Sinister religion) they were mutilated, tortured and beaten to death.

St. Joseph's was crowded. Nan and Angel stood shoulder to shoulder perspiring in the heat despite the whirring of fans mounted on the cathedral's columns. At the conclusion of the service the congregation gave Archbishop Joseph Ngô Quang Kiệt a huge round of applause. Hanoi has made his removal a condition for having diplomatic relations with the Vatican. He is accused of taking advantage of his parishioners' beliefs and their 'low awareness of the law' to instigate unrest. The 'unrest' referred to is prayer. In spite of continued harassment the Archbishop has defied the authorities and supports those 'who suffer oppression, expropriation of land, churches and cemeteries, along with gratuitous violence.'

Ho Chi Minh encouraged the Vietnamese Catholics to fight alongside the Viet Minh against the French, but turned against them as soon as he secured their allegiance. After Dien Bien Phu 5,000 catholic priests and missionaries were arrested by the communists for 'lack of vigilance' and executed or sent to re-education camps. Churches and cathedrals were turned into storerooms for agricultural and farm implements. Because religion diverts attention to a life hereafter, discouraging fighting a revolutionary war for temporal gain, Ho replaced religious instruction in schools with Marxism.

Although the old suspicion of Catholicism remains the Church enjoys a limited religious freedom. While the Holy See and Vietnam have no diplomatic relations there are moves towards a rapprochement of sorts. Communists may no longer believe that religion is the escape of the oppressed by the upper classes, but remain convinced that there is no higher authority than the Party. Because the Party's policies are all embracing and Absolute, it alone can move humanity, and each nation's humanity, towards the goal of justice and freedom. The fallacy of this claim rests on the failure of any government or political organization to provide a new and more solid base for the development of man's humanity.

18

After the service Nan and Angel walked back to Nan's home in West Lake, an upmarket area following the lake's 17 kilometre shore line. Nan's house was a spacious modern two story villa surrounded by a high wall. With the exception of the back garden and pool, which were overlooked by an apartment block, the house was private and sheltered from the street.

Over lunch Nan told Angel how she and her family were helicoptered out of Saigon and the fate of those who could not leave after the communist victory.

'As soon as the communists entered Saigon they started indoctrinating people in Ho Ch Minh's revolutionary ideas about freedom and independence Under a portrait of Ho, hectoring cadres tried to outdo each other, lecturing for four or five hours on the same topic: Ho's inspiring leadership of the Communist Party and his passionate devotion to the cause of his people. At half past four every morning loudspeakers burst into life with martial music, while a metallic voice called out socialist slogans and Party directives. Books and music were banned. Afraid to be seen with incriminating evidence, bonfires burned in gardens all over Saigon, filling the air with the ashes of Balzac and Hans Christian Anderson. Anyone who failed to respond to the new world of communism was arrested and subject to 're-education' or banished to one of the 'New

Economic Zones', uninhabited mountainous forests or areas devastated by defoliants.

'Most of the million people forcibly relocated to these areas never returned. The camps were as savage as those setup by Stalin and Mao Zeong. Workers were shackled in the sun without water and locked in tiger cages. Others were taken into mine fields and told to sweep the ground with their hands. Many of them were wounded, killed, or blown up by mines. Apart from their inhumanity, these communist gulags worked against their own interests by destroying the lives of thousands of skilled people needed for the country's recovery.

'Anyone who could get away did so, although it was an illegal act under the communist government. The 'boat people' made up a large part of those fearing retribution once it was found out that they had fought against the North during the war. They risked their lives on small, old and crudely built boats to escape. Thousands waded into the sea, among them mothers clutching babies. Many drowned or were trampled to death as they fought to reach barges and fishing boats; sometimes South Vietnamese soldiers shot civilians to make room for themselves.

'After journeys of up to 6 months, those who were lucky succeeded in reaching Hong Kong or the shores of neighbouring countries, though some countries, such as Malaya, turned the boat people away even if they did manage to land. The unlucky ones, an estimated of 400,000 out of the millions that fled, died at sea through drowning and disease, and many were attacked by pirates and murdered or sold into slavery and prostitution.'

Nan's own experience of her last days in Saigon was less harrowing. Thanks to her father's work as an interpreter at the American Embassy, she and her family were among those airlifted out of Saigon. Over a span of eighteen hours the Americans carried out the largest helicopter evacuation on record. While the Communists were firing rockets at Saigon airport, a fleet of seventy marine helicopters shuttled back and forth between the city and aircraft carriers off shore. Between them they lifted more than a thousand Americans and nearly six thousand Vietnamese out of the beleaguered capital, two thousands of them from the American compound.

Her family settled in Santa Ana in Southern California. Nan's mother resumed her career as a doctor. Her father became a Court Interpreter with the Superior Court of California. Nan met her future husband after graduating from college at a function sponsored by the Vietnamese Community of Orange County. Although Tien was twenty years her senior, they fell in love and were married. It was not a courtship of high romance, but the marriage was happy.

Tien was a successful entrepreneur, importing garments and textiles from Southeast Asia. He had fled Vietnam after partition, but returned in 1988 after they were married under the aegis of a United Nations Development Program to help the government make the transition from a centrally planned economy to a 'market-oriented' socialism. He visited Hanoi again in 1991 as part of a California Trade delegation. Tempted by the tax breaks introduced after the US ended its trade embargo, Tien and Nan decided to return to Vietnam and set up business in Hanoi. Quick to see that the wider opening of the economy would turn Vietnam into a favourable market for investors, Tien was among the first American Viet *kieu*, or overseas Vietnamese, to relocate to Vietnam.

In the absence of children, Nan immersed herself in her husband's ever growing empire. By the time of Tien's death their company had become one of the largest textile companies in Vietnam. It had not been easy. Vietnam is among the most complex start-up environments in the world. While the country is home to a stable credit environment, and obtaining capital is a relatively smooth process, one is faced with bribery and corruption and bureaucratic hurdles setup by every government department.

Angel did not want to get drawn into the subject of her husband's death, but when Nan asked if he had heard about his murder he could not avoid it.

'I saw it mentioned in the Viet Nam News.'

'Tien was not held up and robbed as the papers said. He was murdered by Kai's Security Service. No one knows the identity of the man they arrested. There was no trial, and no court sentence. This is how it is done here. Just an announcement that the killer has been found guilty and executed.'

'Was your husband against the government?'

'No. He wanted reform. He had discussions with friends in the Politburo about rising income inequality, corruption, and the spiralling budget deficit. But they were not planning a coup or anything subversive. Tien was killed as a warning to those in favour of a more democratic form of government.'

Nan picked up a copy of the Hanoi Times from the table and passed it to Angel. 'You might like to ask Kai what became of the thousands of people that General Quang and the police have arrested.'

General Tran Dai Quang reported to the National Assembly that from June 2012 until November 2015, "The police have received, arrested, and dealt with 1,410 cases involving 2,680 people who violated national security" He said, "During this same period, opposition persons have illegally established more than 60 groups and organizations in the name of democracy and human rights, which have about 350 participants from 50 cities and provinces." According to Gen Quang's report, the police have "timely prevented activities of opposition persons in the country who stirred and agitated the people to gather, march, and protest against the Party and the State. [The police] have actively attacked against [opposition groups] in the political realm and divided and isolated leading figures in order to prevent them from gathering forces in the from of 'civil social organizations '" Gen. Quang insisted that the tasks for the police include "preventing any plan to form and publicize domestic opposition political organizations, as well as activities that form and publicize illegal groups and organizations on the Internet.

'Anyway,' Nan said, 'they are fighting a losing battle.'

'In what way?'

'People are buying up mobile devices at a rate exceeding Vietnam's population. You can buy cell phones for as little as $20. There are now more than 130 million of these devices in the country. It is undermining the Party's monopoly on information. People can know what is actually going on now.'

'Why not the papers?'

'The law explicitly states that the press is the voice of the Party. From time to time journalists were encouraged to expose corruption and mismanagement, but then found themselves under investigation and arrested for doing so.

'Foreign journalists who are here for a short time meet few difficulties. It is not the same for foreign correspondents. They must live in Hanoi. If they want to leave the city they must advise the Ministry of Culture and Information and are accompanied by a 'minder.' Their phones and emails are almost certainly tapped and their movements monitored. The crackdown on free speech and human rights activists in Vietnam is second only to that of Chinese government under Xi Jinping.'

19

Angel received a call from Kai a few days after the warehouse affray saying he had some news that might interest him.

There is a deep gulf between what a man is and what he represents, between what he is as an individual and his persona as bearer of an office determined by his predecessors. To outsiders Kai assumed the role expected of a high ranking minister and Head of Security. Until the arson attack on the warehouse his relationship with Angel was similarly inclined. But since then the two men had come closer and their conversations more open and relaxed.

Kai stood up and smiled. 'How is Mrs Tien?'

'She's well.' Angel paused. 'You are mistaken about her husband. He did meet with some of your colleagues. But there was no talk of undermining the government or setting up an opposition Party. They discussed economic reform, corruption and unemployment. Tien may have drafted something to that effect, but it was a discussion paper, nothing more.'

Kai nodded. 'I was against his death. I thought it was unnecessary.'

'And you could not prevent it?'

Kai shrugged. 'We are not here to talk about Tien. Another time perhaps. I think you will be more interested in what I have to tell you. The men we arrested at the warehouse were working for Ha Tay.'

'Who is Ha Tay?'

'He's a gang leader in the far North. We've known about him for some time.'

'Another Nam Cam, with the police in his pocket?'

'Not quite. But there are people who do not want to see him arrested.'

'Do you know who they are?'

'We think so. But we have no proof. Government ministers have more power than your politicians in the West. They are not restrained by the rules and limitations of their office. Occasionally this freedom is misused for personal gain. You mentioned Nam Can. If you are familiar with the case you will remember that Quoc Huy, my Vice-minister for Police, was tried and convicted. But we must tread carefully. Arrests at this level are damaging to the party.

To carry out Ho Chi Minh's program of unification called for a political system very different from Western democracy and the judiciary which we inherited from the French.'

'Was that wise? The *Code Civil* has a written constitution that would have put an end to many of the abuses that plague this country.'

'The principle tenet of the *Code Civil* is that every person is equal before the law. This was certainly not the case during the French colonization of Vietnam. In fact our judiciary is more true to the Code than the French were. Have you spoken to Mrs. Tien about these things?'

'You mean about the French occupation?'

'Yes.'

'No. Not really. Why?'

'She was raised in an affluent southern family of *collaborator*s, Vietnamese who embraced French colonial rule in exchange for favours. Her father taught at a French lycée in Saigon, a signal honour for a 'native' of his generation, and later worked for the Americans. Her mother, unusually liberated for a Vietnamese woman, went to medical school in Paris. In 1954, back in Saigon, she entered the resistance against the Vietcong, serving as a covert South Vietnamese agent while she practised medicine.'

'Why are you telling me this?'

'While we were fighting for our independence in the jungles the Tien's enjoyed a French lifestyle in a comfortable villa. They were spared the horrors of war and seeing our towns and villages turned into bloody battlegrounds. As for the *Code Civil*, it did not apply to the Vietnamese. You've been to *Maison Central,* the French prison. You've seen the displays: the cruelty perpetrated against the nationalists who were fighting for independence.

'Because our judicial system is responsible to the leadership of the Communist Party, the administration of justice is largely in the hands of the Security Police. Unfortunately Hồ Chí Minh's policies ideas were not systematised during his lifetime As a result communist cadres without any legal training were appointed judges and justices, and decrees of Parry leaders were interpreted literally and made law. '

Angel understood that Kai was excusing the aberrations of Vietnam's military tribunals and people's courts. And more significantly, the difficulty of calling the leadership to account. Not wanting to engage Kia in a discussion on the harmful effects of dressing up ideological orders as normal police regulations, Angel returned to the subject of Ha Tay.

'You said that Ha Tay organized the arson attack, but that he was not the blackmailer.'

'Tay was following orders. He is a petty criminal. He does not know about international accounts. Also he would not voluntarily engage in blackmail. Although we have lifted the death penalty for blackmail it carries a long sentence. It is not something he would risk.'

'Who stands behind Tay?'

'The most likely person is Ninh Moi.'

'Ninh Moi?'

'He is a successful businessman, and one of Tien's competitors. Like Tien he made his money in textiles. He has factories in Hanoi and Ho Chi Minh City. We know that he was bidding on the same contract as Tien. The contract was worth tens of thousands of dollars to the successful bidder. It is possible that after Tien's death, having lost the contract, he decided to blackmail Tien's wife.

'But you have no evidence.'

'Not at this time.'

'So we are back to square one.'

'Not quite. We have a suspect. We will keep an eye on him.'

'Surely you can let Moi know that he is under suspicion. Unless the man is a fool it should be enough to stop him from trying this stunt again.'

'Unfortunately it is not as easy as that. Moi is married to our President's sister.'

Angel gave a silent chuckle. Another circus act of things not appearing as they seem.

'This has to be a 'silent enquiry'. For reasons I have explained, the Party's senior members are not subject to the usual checks and controls. Although Moi is not a minister his relationship to the President gives him a certain immunity.'

'Time,' Angel said, with a wry smile, 'to bring in Aquino.'

'We are not the KGB.'

Angel let the remark pass. The only difference between the two State security organizations was that the CPV used a contract killer whereas the Soviets use in-house assassins.

'We will not use Aquino's services again if we can help it,' Kai added.

Angel was not sure that Aquino could be 'retired'. Killing was in his blood. The CIA and the Soviets used mind control techniques: hypnosis, electrotherapy, and drugs to erase or scramble their operative's memory. But these tools and techniques were not available to Kai or work in the case of a pathological killer.

'Aquino has become a danger to himself and to others. You could put him on a plane to Manila.'

'I'll consider it,' Kai said. 'But let us return to Moi. For the time being it is better that he thinks he is above suspicion and immune from prosecution. Given time he will entrap himself, such people always do.' Kai paused, and then said, 'With your help we can speed up this process.'

Angel smiled. 'I'm weary of your offers to help.'

Kai smiled and nodded. 'We are no longer interested in Tien's affairs. If you agree, it will be voluntarily.'

'What do you have in mind?'

'Arms are being smuggled in from China. We have found caches of weapons in Sa Pa and in Cao Bang. We think Moi is behind it. The calibre of the rifles matches those used by Tay's men. Tay might have his weapons elsewhere, but we think not.'

'Why would the President's son-in-law smuggle arms into Vietnam?'

'There is a good reason for it. But I prefer not to say more at this time.'

'You would like me to meet him?'

'He'll be attending a conference at the Hanoi Business Club next week. I will see that you are invited.'

'And...?'

'You might learn if he is in interested in buying arms.'

'Mr. Kai you delight in casting me in roles that I would rather not play.'

'I know you will think of something Mr. Angel.'

'Very well. But I am doing this for Mrs. Tien.'

Angel could have pressed Kai to explain Tien's murder since Tien's affairs were no longer of interest. Reading between the lines the instruction to eliminate Tien must have come from the president since he was the only minister in the CPV senior to Kai. As Nan had predicted, the bitter power struggle within the Politburo between the reformers and the hardliners meant that Kai was bound to act as the president asked, in spite of his reservations, as a warning to those against Ho's Marxist policies.

'Mr Angel, before you leave.'

Kai opened a drawer and drew out Angel's passport. 'Your passport, Mr. Angel. You are a free man. I hope you decide to stay in Vietnam. But we will not stand in your way if you decide to leave.'

Angel acknowledged the return of his passport with a nod of his head and a quietly spoken 'thank you'. His passport was no longer an issue. In his mind he would have no further need of it.

20

'Aquino? This is Angel.'

'Yes.'

'I've spoken to Kai. He has no objection to you leaving Vietnam. It's worth considering.'

'I know too much.'

'It's not an issue,' Angel said.

A pause.

'You see a lot of Kai.' It sounded like an accusation.

'Not a lot. He returned my passport.'

'You're leaving Vietnam?'

'No.'

Aquino grunted.

'You're working for him?' Another expressionless question.

Angel paused. 'No.'

Aquino picked up the hesitation. 'You sure?'

'You mean the business with the warehouse? I did that for Mrs. Tien.'

Silence from Aquino.

'Think about Manila,' Angel said, and put down the phone. He hoped he had said enough for Aquino to think about leaving..

Kai, along with other members of the politburo had a villa in Ba Dinh, near Ho Chi Minh's mausoleum. The house was set behind high walls, and guarded twenty-four hours a day.

Anyone caught loitering nearby was arrested. But someone with Aquino's skills could always find the time and the place for a fatal shot.

Kai's assassination did not bear thinking about.

21

Kai had suggested in a moment of relaxed conversation that Angel should visit the Military History Museum.

The shape and quality of all wars are the same: the surrender of reason to violence. But the War Museum is more than a display of man's inventiveness for killing. It covers a crucial period of Vietnamese history from the 1930s with the formation of the old Indochinese Communist Party to the present day.

The Museum occupies a 10,000 square meter site in a prominent position in Dien Bien Phu Street opposite Lenin's statue. Lenin looks confidently across to the entrance of the museum and the mangled wreckage of a B-52 bomber at the foot of a tree. The cavernous courtyard is full of weaponry, foremost of which is a Russian MiG-21 fighter, alongside one of the tanks that crashed through the gates of the Presidential Palace in Saigon in 1975.

The main exhibition starts on the second floor and runs chronologically from the 'People's War' against the French to the collapse of Saigon. Despite the heavy propaganda overlay, the room-sized models of major battles against the French and Americans are impressive. The accompanying archive footage of the Viet Minh hauling artillery up mountain slopes and wounded marines being dragged into helicopters is a stark reminder that war has only one end in view, the taking of human life.

Angel was back in Kai's office forty-eight hours after their last meeting. It was now very familiar: the black and white photographs, the book shelves holding Das *Kapital*, Kai's citations, the big desk and the comfortable chairs. After a minute or two Kai got to the point and said that he had set up a meeting for Angel with Ninh Moi.

'I've spoken to the Chairman of the Business Club. He'll introduce you to Moi. I told him you were here on our invitation, working with our procurement department.'

'Good.'

'Have you decided how to approach him?'

'Yes. If he takes the bait I'll need some information about your armament program, and other confidential information.'

'I'll see to that. Anything else.'

'None of your people must know that we are working together. Moi was sure to have his spies in Kai's ministry. Any whisper of Kai's collusion would bring Angel's plans to a halt.

'Agreed.'

The business with Moi settled, Kai asked Angel if had visited the Army Museum. 'It chronicles our national history from the 1930s to the present day,' Kai said.

'I took your advice.'

'And?'

'The sight of so much machinery engineered for death was depressing. It reminded me that we know more about war than we know about peace; more about killing than we know about living.'

'The fascination with technology has its dangers,' Kai admitted. 'It turns our interest away from people and nature. Man becomes part of the total machinery that he controls, and to some extent is controlled by. It was Marx who brought this to man's attention. He not only foresaw the dangers of technology, but more significantly, saw its roots in capitalism. Capitalism drives the economy towards increased specialization, which in turn furthers the division of labour. The more the division of labour there is in a society the greater the exploitation - and likely use of violence.'

Angel did not argue the point. Kai knew very well that market forces were driving Vietnam towards a capitalist economy – creating a class-system in the process leading to economic domination, exploitation and oppression. In the race for wealth, communism pays no more heed to Marx than capitalism.

'War, for all its suffering, is perhaps the only way of putting an end to political abnormalities like ISIL. It is a tragedy is that people must always die to make the world a safer and better place.'

'Again, Marx understood better than anyone that war was needless suffering. More than the cruelty, waste and misery of war, he hated the cause of war: the structural injustices of an economic system based on private ownership.'

Angel acknowledged Kai's words with a doubtful shrug.

'Neither Soviet communism nor Chinese Maoism has created an economic system that moves us towards equality. There will always be divisions of labour. People differ in their possessions of native talent, opportunities, initiative and resources. Freedom is more important than equality. The attempt to realise equality endangers freedom. If freedom is lost, there will not be equality among those that are free.'

Angel had given a stock answer in defence of capitalism, fully aware that neither communism, capitalism, Marxism – nor any other 'ism' was the answer to the problem of suffering and evil.

Before Angel's 'glimpse' of a more far reaching reality than a United Nations or a World Government he believed that only such organizations were capable of moving humanity towards justice and freedom. But the short-sighted practicality of such organizations, and their failure to offer a universally accessible solution to the problem of violence, demonstrated that only in a limited fashion can reason and common sense have any real bearing on the conduct of human affairs.

22

When Angel was on his own he liked to stroll through the congested square mile of narrow streets in the Old Quarter. That it existed at all was due to a decade of repressive communist government that kept the country at a standstill. Nothing like the old centre of Hanoi survives anywhere else in Southeast Asia. By the time Vietnam's economy began to pick up and developers started thinking about tearing down the crowded and cramped houses, the World Heritage Organization listed the Old Quarter as a world heritage site that must be saved.

Not everyone takes kindly to the jigsaw of narrow streets, chaotic traffic and patchwork architecture. Fascinating at any time, the Quarter took on a special atmosphere after the evening traffic died down. Life spilled out onto the sidewalks. Shops and stalls blazed with colour, and the babble of voices turned every street and alleyway into a market.

Nan preferred the quieter walk around Hamm Kiem Lake. Just before nightfall the water took on a strange iridescence, as if illuminated from below. It was after one such walk, following a meeting with Kai that Angel told Nan that he had agreed to meet with Ninh Moi.

'Why?'

'Kai thought I might like to meet some of Hanoi's leading businessmen. Kai is not such a hard-line communist as I thought. He knows there are structural defects in the way it works. He also said that he was not responsible for your husband's death.'

'You believe him?'

'Yes'. There was no need to tell Nan that it was an executive order.

Angel turned the conversation back to Moi. 'I'm meeting Moi at the Hanoi Business Club.'

'My husband stopped going there. He said that it was a waste of time. Everyone knew that Kai's spies were in the room. Occasionally someone would complain about the red tape and the corruption. But for the most part no one said anything that could be taken as a criticism of the government. But why Moi of all people?'

'Do you know him?'

'Yes. Not well. He's one of our biggest competitors. My husband didn't trust him.'

'Why?'

Nan shrugged. 'There is a saying in Vietnamese, *Lời nói không đi đôi với việc làm.*'

'Meaning?'

'The man hides the truth behind his back.'

'You said he was a competitor.'

'He has an import export business like our own. Because of his connections – he is married to the president's sister, he gets all the government contracts, even though our prices are more competitive.'

'What else do you know about him?

'Does the name 'Kok Ksor' mean anything?'

'No.'

'Kok Ksor is a member of FULRO (Front Unifié de la Lutte des Races Opprimées). It is a nationalist movement calling for an autonomous homeland for the Montagnards. In Vietnam it has become a fragmented guerrilla group opposed to all forms of Vietnamese rule.

'Who are the Montagnards?'

'The indigenous peoples of the Central Highlands. The Vietnamese refer to them pejoratively as Moi, or savages. They have no real status or human rights. They have suffered the same mistreatment and exploitation as the Australian aboriginal and African Bushmen.'

'And Kok Ksor?'

'He runs the South Carolina-based Montagnard Foundation. He is a thorn in the side of the VCP because his foundation finances the demonstrations mounted by the highland minorities.

'The Montagnards, or *Degar* as they call themselves, have had a long and troubled history in Vietnam. Under French rule they found themselves dispossessed from their traditional hunting and agricultural grounds and forced to labour in plantations. Then during the Vietnam War the Americans conducted massive bombing raids along the Lao and Chinese borders, the Degar's ancestral homeland. Two hundred thousand Degar were killed, and nearly all their villages destroyed.'

'War has no centre. Its periphery can be just as dangerous as the front line. Did the Degar support the Viet Cong?'

'No, and Hanoi has never forgiven them. American and French missionaries converted the hill tribes to Catholics and Protestants, which is why they fought alongside the Americans against the Viet Cong. In retaliation the Communists launched one of the worst atrocities of the war against them. Two battalions of Viet Cong launched a 'vengeance' attack on the hamlet of Dak Son killing 250 men, women and children. Six hundred troops marched into the village using flamethrowers. Families were incinerated inside their own homes. Houses not destroyed by flamethrowers were destroyed with grenades. It was unpardonable.

'After the war things got worse. The scale of Vietnamese attacks on the Montagnards reached genocidal proportions. In the years following the fall of Saigon the North Vietnamese slaughter over 200,000 Degar. The Americans won't criticise Hanoi for the persecution of the Montagnards, or for implementing a discriminatory policy against them (banning their languages and forbidding anything to be written in Montagnard including the Bible), because it wants Vietnam as an ally against China. The Degar did not get the support after the war they were promised by the State Department, but rely on aid from private organizations like the STMP (Save the Montagnard People) and Kok Ksor's foundation.'

'What does this have to do with Moi?'

'Moi went to school with Kok Ksor. He is Kok Ksor's man in Vietnam. He keeps a low profile when it comes to politics, but Bai, my husband said he was behind the protests and armed uprisings that erupt periodically.'

'How did he know that?'

'My husband met Kok Ksor when we lived in America. He asked Bai for money to support the revolution for an independent homeland and told him that Moi was his agent.'

'Why would Moi risk everything to secure a breakaway province for the Montagnards? The last thing the communists want is a fractured Vietnam.'

'Moi doesn't care about Vietnam. He wants a presidential role for himself. If the Degar secured a partial independence from Hanoi, Moi would be a front runner for the post of Chief Executive. He's trusted by the President, and because he was born in Lao Cai he would be acceptable to the Montagnards. He hides his ties with Ksor's foundation, while working behind the scenes to bring about a Degar state. Last year when the army was brought in to quell a riot in the northern delta area, Moi told Pham Binh Minh (the Minister of Foreign Affairs), that Kok Ksor's relatives were behind the uprising. Subsequently five of Kok's relatives were arrested, including Kok's mother. Afterwards the Foreign Ministry spokesman, Le Dung, said that Ksor and his family had admitted that they were guilty of "terrorist activities." This was not true. Kok's family were under virtual house arrest. They would not have done anything to incriminate themselves. But it cleared Moi of any association with Kok Ksor and the Montagnard Foundation - which is considered a criminal organization in Vietnam.'

'So Ninh Moi is turncoat.'

'More than that. He's very ambitious and unscrupulous. I can't think why Kai would want you to meet him.'

23

The Hanoi Business Club is in My Din, near the Lomonoxop High School, a twenty minute drive from the centre of Hanoi. Although Kia had referred to the meeting as a conference, it was more an informal get together of local business men. People sat or stood in small groups, complaining about the stream of documentation required for importing and exporting as well as other difficulties associated with doing business in Vietnam.

As soon as he entered the club Angel was recognized by the Chairman and introduced to Moi.

'I'm told you are working for our Ministry of Public Security,' Moi said, when he and Angel were alone together.

'Not exactly. I am advising the Minister on weapon systems, primarily for homeland security.'

'Then you know all about armaments?'

'With respect to light infantry weapons, yes.'

'Are you a personal friend of the Minister?'

'No. I was seconded from the SAS.'

Moi asked Angel about his time in Hanoi, and then, unexpectedly, if he was being paid generously for his work.

'Not particularly. My salary is paid by the SAS, in addition to which I get a small overseas allowance.'

'Then you would not be averse to supplementing your income while you are here?'

Angel smiled. 'No, not at all. I have time to spare.'

Moi nodded. 'Good. Mr. Angel, I think we can do business together. Let us talk privately. Tomorrow, midday, at the Hilton?'

'Very well.'

Angel left the club soon afterwards. Although not drawn to Moi, the man had a restless energy and self-confidence. Physically he resembled General Vo Nguyen Giap, the military leader of the Viet Minh resistances against the Japanese whose photographs adorned the walls of the Club. Of medium height, Moi had an intelligent face, with evenly spaced eyes and full lips. A man quite evidently sure of himself.

24

The Hilton is in the centre of the upmarket Hoan Kiem district, within walking distance of Hanoi's central business district. Behind its stunning French exterior, modelled on the Palais Garnier, the older of Paris' two opera houses, is a traditionally furnished hotel, comfortable and conservative.

Reception told Angel that Mr. Ninh Moi was waiting for him in the Executive Lounge on the 7th floor. When Moi saw Angel he stood up and asked Angel to be seated. On the table was a pot of green tea, two cups, and a plate of Vietnamese butter biscuits.

Moi got straight down to business. 'Mr. Angel, how would you bring a large quantity of firearms into Vietnam?'

'I wouldn't try. I've been to most of the country's border and customs posts. And while the staff appear to be less than diligent, nothing the size of a crate would pass through without being inspected. You could smuggle a small cache of rifles into the country along jungle tracks, but it would be risky. Most of these routes are known to the authorities.'

Moi nodded. 'Before we return to this question, may I ask what arms and munitions you have recommended.'

'7.62mm automatic rifles. Either the FN SCAR, a Belgium designed rifle manufactured in the States, or a Kalashnikov. Both are accurate and have a good service life. The key factor with regards to hit probability is not the rifle or ammunition but sighting equipment. The best is the Swarovski, but procurement may find it too expensive. Do you want me to continue?'

'No Mr. Angel, I'm sure of your judgement. Whatever you have proposed would be suitable for our use. If we can overcome the problem of entry, can arms and ammunition be obtained without a license?'

'You can buy pretty much anything you like: Glocks, Berettas, PPKs, AK-47s, even grenades, without a licence and have them shipped anywhere in the world.'

'How?'

'Through an on-line resource for weapons. It can be accessed using TOR, a software program developed by the US Navy that directs Internet traffic through a worldwide network of more than seven thousand relays to conceal the user's location and identity. TOR routes your connection through a sprawling maze of encrypted PGP keys making it almost impossible to trace.'

'What about delivery?'

'Unless you can arrange your own transport, and in your case, this would mean an aircraft and landing strip, TOR would not help. A dealer will strip a weapon down to its parts and ship it in pieces. An Ak 47 might arrive over the course of two weeks packed in shielded packages disguised to look like any other products that requires self-assembly. But it is still a risky business. Interpol scans the "The Armoury" and other vendors of illegal arms. If they identify the buyer he will be arrested.'

'Then that's out of the question. The arms I want must be delivered as normal cargo. How can that be done, Mr Angel?'

'The weak link in the chain of procurement, from the standpoint of security, is the delivery of the shipment from warehouse to its destination.'

Angel paused.

'Hanoi's recent spat with Beijing revealed that Vietnam's armed services are ill-equipped to meet any serious threat. In addition to six fast attack submarines, missiles and anti-personnel mines, the government has placed a large order of small arms and ammunition The first consignment has already arrived. The second, which includes 1000 semi-automatic rifles, will leave Russia in a few weeks.'

'Are you suggesting that we hijack the cargo?'

'I'm not suggesting anything. I'm simply saying that once the shipment has been offloaded it is vulnerable until it has been delivered to its destination.'

'It sounds too easy.'

'Not so easy Mr. Moi. You need to have someone on the inside. Someone who has access to all the relevant details: the name of the vessel carrying the arms, the date and port of delivery, the location and number of the bonded warehouse. You also need to know what additional security arrangements, if any, have been made, and the significance of the stencilled markings on each crate. If you had these details, and were able to gain entry into the warehouse, the rest should be straightforward.'

'Are you are in a position to give me that information.'

'Yes.'

'And the fee?'

$50,000 paid into my UK account.'

'Agreed.'

25

For someone accustomed to the highs and lows of battle, for whom a settled existence had been an anathema, Angel was surprised to find that living with Nan was great deal more exciting than the emotionally charged drama of combat. Although deception and intrigue, so favoured by the security police, had no place in his life with Nan, he was in favour of ending Moi's immunity from prosecution.

Nan asked Angel if Moi had mentioned the Degars when they met.

'No.'

Nan shrugged. 'As I said, he has no interest in the welfare of the Hill Tribes. He uses them to realise his political ambitions. Ksor speaks out for the Montargards; but Moi wants an armed uprising to compel Hanoi to concede to a separate homeland. He is banking on the fact that voices all around the world are calling for governments to recognize the rights of their indigenous peoples. Vietnam has a poor press with regards to its treatment of its minorities. The more unrest, the greater the international pressure on the CPV to grant the Degars their independence.'

'It's a pipe dream,' Angel said. 'Moi seriously miscalculated if he thinks a show of force will persuade the communists to surrender territory to the Degar. Even if Moi were successful in launching an armed insurrection it would be a toy war for the Vietnamese army.'

'He will get his war if he wants it,' Nan said. 'There are guerrilla groups among the Degar who are prepared to fight. But without weapons, they are a spent force.'

'Even so, you need more than guns to mount a revolution. People have to be at odds with their political leaders and feel that they are being oppressed.'

'But that is how the Degar feel. The last report from Human Rights Watch described a massive crackdown by Hanoi in the Central Highlands. Hundreds of troops went on a manhunt for villagers involved in protests. People were forced to hide in village graves or pits in the forest to escape capture. If the Degar had guns, there would be a civil war.'

26

Angel told Kai about his meeting with Moi and the substance of their agreement.

'It seems that our confrontation with China have come at an opportune time, at least as far as Moi is concerned,' Kai said. 'China has become increasingly aggressive in the South China Sea. Xi Jinping is claiming sovereignty over the Paracels and the Spratlys. He maintains the China's rights over the islands goes back centuries. China issued a map in 1947 showing the two island chains falling within its territory. But China never claimed sovereignty over the islands before 1947. We have documents to prove that Vietnam actively ruled the Paracels and the Spratlys since the 17th century.'

'Compared to China's aggressive claims the business with Moi seems very unimportant.'

'Yes, but the last thing we want is an armed uprising. Of all wars that a country can be cursed with a civil war is the worst. Our war with the South still carries unhealed wounds and tensions. Did Moi believe your story?'

'I'm sure of it. Give me another day or two and I'll let you know Moi's plans exactly. In the meantime I need the following information.' Angel passed Kai a list of questions regarding the procurement, storage, and delivery of the arms and munitions.

'If this ruse is successful I hope you will ignore his s presidential connections and prosecute.'

'Moi is a little man, who has become a big man, and now wants to become Tsar of the hill tribes. Unfortunately his position and wealth allow him a certain immunity over and beyond his stature as a person.'

'You would not be having these problems with Moi if the CPV had treated the Degar fairly. The government has expropriated their ancestral lands, made arbitrary arrests and denied them religious freedom. I've seen a paper published by the U.N. Sub-Commission on human rights. It documents the execution and torture of the Montagnards as well as the burning of their churches, and a bounty for the capture of those who fled to Cambodia. It also said that funds from international aid bodies allocated for family planning programmes had been misused to perform forced sterilisation on Montagnard women.'

'I've seen that report, Mr. Angel. Do you know who the author is?'

'No.'

'Kok Ksor. He is the executive director of the U.S.-based Montagnard Foundation. Its members are a bunch of militant activists with nothing better to do than stir up trouble. They use the nationality and religious card to incite the Montagnards to take up arms against the CPV. Ksor's family have confessed to carrying out Kok's instructions to destabilize relations with the authorities. Under normal circumstance the Degar would be no more than an irritant. But Ksor receives clandestine material support from China in the form of weapons and munitions. If these fall into the hands of the Degar we could have a small war on our hands. On balance, I'm not too concerned with Moi. I am concerned that a flood of arms might ignite old hostilities and garner support for an insurrection. The Degar are hiding their munitions in the mountains near Ban Me Thou, the Montagnard capital. We need to find these arms, stop their illegal entry and end once and for all the idea of an independent homeland.'

'With regards to the munitions, I assume you will put a GPS tracker in each crate.'

'Yes'

'I would also replace the ammunition with bags of sand. The Chinese Type 53 carbines used by the Montagnards are a different calibre to the Russian rifles. Without ammunition the rifles will be useless.'

'Anything else?'

'As I've already said, I would like to see Moi behind bars.'

'The only evidence we have linking him to this operation is the $50,000 he promised you, and even this is not grounds for his arrest. For various reasons we cannot use your testimony. On the other hand if we are successful it will be a huge setback to his plans. Moi is not a fool. He will know that we are watching him. '

'In case you are wondering what I will do with the $50,000 - it is going to the Special Air Service Regimental Association. They will send a 'thank you' letter to Moi in appreciation of his unsolicited generosity.'

27

Working with Kai to prevent a conflict which might easily bring destruction to the Montagards had brought Kai and Angel closer together. There were still areas of disagreement between them, not least Marxism's aggressive atheism that maintained that the State is the only one true reality. Since the Party represents the State, its leaders could claim absolute authority in all matters. This facade of legality justified the communist hierarchy maintaining their private preserves and jealously guarded individual rights – backed up, if necessary, by a vigilant secret police and the threat of labour camps.

There were times when Kai dropped his guard, admitting that while communism has succeeded in making religion a marginal factor in human affairs, it has not succeeded in abolishing hatred or war. It was a small concession, but one that allowed the two men to question each nother and ultimately to understand one another.

If talking brought Kai and Angel closer together, the same could not be said for Aquino. Talking to Aqiono was like talking through a mist to an unknown figure. Words lost their bearing, and isolated from reality. Incapable of identifying with or caring about the emotional pain he caused his victims or their families, conversations with Aquino had a a chilling disregard for human empathy and compassion. His soulless words produced not understanding but alienation.

If Aquino represent the nadir of speech, Moi was not far behind. Talking to Moi called for an adroitness of language that that eschewed veracity. Truth has sometimes to be ruthlessly false, a paradox borne out by the situation in which Angel found him. Ill rehearsed for deception and the use of words for this purpose, talking to Moi neither encouraged good will nor mutual understanding. Angel might have been talking to a cardboard cut out for all the amity it inspired.

Having received the information he needed from Kai, Angel met Moi in his office in Ba Dinh as arranged.

'I suggest you make a note of these things,' Angel said. 'This will be our last meeting. There will be no further exchange between us, in person, by phone, or in writing,'

'I understand.'

'The vessel's name is *Inessa Armand*. It will sail from Vladivostok in two weeks time and arrive in Haipong on the 23rd of this month. It will berth at the Hoang Dieu Terminal. The cargo will be stored in the government bonded warehouse on Cau Ngu Wharf. The rifles, 1000 AK 47's, are packed in crates, 100 rifles in each crate. You can identify the crates by the Izmash logo, a triangle holding an arrow. Ammunition for the rifles will be on 4 pallets. Each pallet carries 48 boxes holding 1680 rounds per box. A trans-positioner for lifting and moving pallets is on site. The warehouse will be locked, but not guarded. As you know security for the port is the responsibility of the Haiphong Port Authority. How you get in and out of the terminal is your business. It is not something I can help you with.'

'Very good, Mr. Angel. The port's Guard Team know us. We export containers of textiles almost every week. Our trucks will not be searched. I don't expect any problems.'

'I've done my part Mr. Moi, now I expect you to do yours. Here are my bank details.'

'I will attend to it.'

Angel got to his feet, and shook hands with Moi. The next act belonged to Kai.

28

Because of Angel's curiosity to see the Hill Tribes for himself, Nan arranged a trip that would take them to Sa Pa on the Vietnam-Chinese border. Angel had first heard about Vietnam's most mountainous province from Madam Hu, who said that Ho Chi Minh had hidden from the French in the Pac Bo Caves near Sa Pa. But neither Angel nor Nan were interested in seeing Ho's wooden bed or the limestone formations that Ho named Karl Marx, but to simply enjoy a week away from the busy littleness that called on their time when at home.

If Angel had been told that he was 'living in sin' by cohabiting with a married woman he would have dismissed the remark as meaningless. Their love for each other had long since moved beyond considerations of merely personal satisfactions and interests. It was the origin and source of the lovingness that coloured their thoughts and feelings, their hopes and fears, their joys and sorrows. So intimate were their avowals that both knew that their feelings for one another would extend over time, even a life-time.

On the evening before they left for Sa Pa, Angel received another pressing call from Aquino. It was the last person he wished to see or hear from at this time

'It's Aquino.'

'Yes.'

'Lai's bar. Usual time. I'll expect you.'

'It's not convenient.'

'It will have to wait.'

'What's so important?'

'When I see you.'

Aquino had not come to Hanoi to exercise his derringer. Kai had made it clear that he done with extrajudicial killings. Angel guessed that Aquino had dreamt up another harebrained scheme to kill his paymaster. But one could not be sure. It was safer to follow Aquino's twisted thinking than be caught unawares.

Angel had led patrols where the unexpected had to be reckoned with. But there were always clues which alerted one to danger: a bit of broken bark, bruised vegetation, urine traces on a bush. But Aquino did not leave clues. He was a stalking shadow. There would be no warning. Just a bullet in the back of the head.

Aquino sat by himself, a bottle of Mekong Whisky at his elbow. Angel pulled up a chair.

'What's on your mind, Aquino?'

'You've seen a lot of Kai.'

Aquino had raised the same question the last time they met. Only it was not a question. Nor was it a statement. It was an accusation.

'Kai thinks their weaponry needs to be updated. Most of his munitions are left over from the war.' Angel spoke in a matter-of-fact voice, dispelling any notion that their meeting had anything to do with Aquino.

'Why now?'

'It seems that Hanoi is worried about China: the fracas over the oil rig and the controversy over the Parcels and Spratly Islands.'

'Why you?'

'He knows that the SAS has the latest equipment.'

'Is that all?'

'That's all.'

Aquino grunted. 'I hear you are living with Mrs. Tien.'

'Yes.'

Aquino smiled. 'I did you a favour.'

Angel let the remark pass. 'Have you thought any more about the Philippines?'

'I don't trust Kai.'

'If he wanted to stop you from leaving he would have done so.'

Aquino shook his head. 'Kai buried the dead, but I have their names. If I go missing, they get posted. Kai will get dragged to the Hague.'

Aquino had lost touch with reality. The real world was slipping out from under his feet.

'Aquino. Forget Kai. Go home.'

Aquino did not look up.

Angel got to his feet. 'Good-by, Aquino.'

It was the last time they spoke.

29

Sa Pa is in the northwest of Vietnam, dominated by the county's highest mountains. It is approached by road from Lao Cai along the steep, terraced hillside of the Hoang Lien Son mountain range. Angel and Nan took the sleeper coach on the overnight train from Hanoi, arriving at Sa Pa early next morning. Forty kilometres and ninety minutes later they reached the Victoria Hotel perched dramatically on the western edge of a high plateau.

Angel learned of the raid on the Montagnard's arms dump when they arrived in Sa Pa. It was headline news in the *Thanh Nien Daily*. Quoting Kai the paper reported that the Security Forces had had averted a full scale insurrection and that an arsenal had been found in a cave near Lao Cai. The weapons were to be used against the Vietnamese by FULRO guerrillas in their on-going struggle for independence. Because most of the weapons were Chinese and smuggled into Vietnam by Chinese agents, President Xi Jinping was accused of war-mongering, in line with his gunboat diplomacy in the South China Sea. There had been a bloody shootout and arrests made. Moi's name was not mentioned.

The morning after the raid the streets of SA Pa were crowded with Montagnards carrying placards calling for the Vietnamese to leave the highlands and to release those who had been imprisoned. Later in the day on Radio Vietnam a spokesman for the Ministry of Foreign Affairs, Le Dzun, denied reports that the security forces had killed a number of people during the raid, a sure sign that lives had been lost.

Lao Cai was an obvious site for an arms dump. It was just three miles from the Chinese border and a popular route for smugglers heading to Kunming via the Hekou Bridge border gate. The town was almost totally destroyed by the Chinese in 1979 when Deng Xiao Ping sent in 200,000 troops to 'teach Vietnam a lesson' for invading Cambodia. To-day Lao Cai is little more than a railhead for Sa Pa and a popular route into China for travelers heading to Kunming.

Sa Pa did not escape Deng Xiao Ping's abortive invasion. Having lost 20,000 men and been driven back into China by the Vietnamese after just two weeks, the Chinese methodically blew up every building they could before withdrawing. The old wooden market with its arched doorways and tiled roof has been replaced with an unsightly concrete building. But on the weekends it bursts into life with Hmong women in their distinctive conical hats and brightly colored clothes. Their hands and arms stained from the indigo leaves used to make the dyes that colour their clothing, they clamour round helpless tourists hawking their hats and bags and tribal jewellery. Say 'thuốc phiên' and hands will reach into embroidered indigo-blue waistcoats for sticks of opium concealed in matchboxes. More than two dozen foreigners are facing the death penalty in Vietnam for possessing opium bought from the Hmong in Sa Pa and the surrounding villages.

Before returning to Hanoi, Nan took Angel to a Montargard church service in Cat Cat, a village below Sa Pa in the Muong Valley. A two mile walk from the hotel, Cat Cat is a huddle of wooden houses hidden by fruit trees and bamboo where chickens and pot bellied pigs scavenge among trailing pumpkin vines. Because the 'church' was mistaken for a barn it had escaped the attention of the authorities. There was nothing to identify the building as a church because the District People's Committee had prohibited the erection of any symbol that could draw attention to its function.

Although the service was spoken in Rade, the language of most Montagnards, the elements were familiar, culminating in the taking of communion. In a country where 80% of the population consider themselves to be non-religious the little church was surprisingly full. Clearly the age old questions that are beyond the power of science to answer had not lost their significance.

On leaving the church the elder gave Nan a copy of Article 5 of Decree 92/2012 ND-CP in the hope that she would sign a petition to save the building from being torn down in the event of its discovery. Article 5 stipulates that a church may not organize religious events, observe rituals, conduct missionary work, or preach unless its restoration was approved twenty years earlier. Any church contravening these regulations is subject to a further decree that mandates its destruction. Since community churches are impossible to date, such ordinances made every village church an illegal structure. It is a fast track way of denying people the right to assemble and worship.

Shamanism is the only alternative to church worship for the Degars. While church and State are undermining their significance, shamans are still found in the more remote villages. Since the shaman is an intermediary or messengers between the human world and the spirit world, he can reassure his audience that their spirits are immortal. Believers are still subject to death as far as it is the physical act of dying, but their impending immortality ensures that death does not have the last word. Hanoi tries to suppress shamanism because it contradicts the Marxist view that man has no reality beyond his material existence. The government's efforts have been largely unsuccessful. Hanoi has found that it is dealing with forces greater than its own.

30

On their return to Hanoi Angel found a letter waiting for him from Kai. Angel rightly guessed that Kai wanted to brief him about the events in Lao Cai.

'The arms dump was much bigger than we thought,' Kai said. 'There were hundreds of Chinese Norinco Type 56 rifles and stockpiles of ammunition. We have increased the border patrol between Lao Cai and Bac Ha. But I don't expect to see much activity. I think we might have finally put an end to smuggling in the area.'

'What about Moi?'

'Moi got his fingers burned. We spread the rumour that he revealed the whereabouts of the cave to ingratiate himself with the authorities. He will have lost the trust and support of the Montagnards. Moi will guess that we have insider knowledge of his role in the affair. I think he will confine himself to his business affairs from now on and forget about his political ambitions.'

'Now that there is no threat of an insurrection, will you give tribes more freedom?'

'Such as?'

'The right to worship as they please?'

'This is a difficult issue. They are abandoning their traditional religious beliefs and practises of spirit worship and converting to evangelical Christianity.'

'Since you consider their traditional beliefs 'superstitious' and 'primitive' I thought you might welcome their conversion.'

'No. Evangelical Christianity is not one of the religions recognized by the Bureau of Religious Affairs.'

'Why not?'

'Because it is not in line with Vietnam's religious traditions and national security.'

'In what way?'

'It was the American evangelical missionaries who urged the Hill Tribes to join the U.S. during the war; the same evangelicals are now sowing discontent among the Montagnards.'

'A church is not a collection of saints. It is like a net cast into the sea that catches all sorts of fish. There may be some malcontents among the Montagnards, but I doubt that the churches are a cover for political activism. When we were in Sa Pa we were told that local officials forced Hmong protestants to recant their faith. They also put pressure on clan elders to tell their extended families to cease practising Christianity.'

'Sometimes local cadres are a little too enthusiastic in carrying out their duties.'

'Including sending believers to a lunatic asylum?'

'You are referring to Than Van Truong.'

'Yes. We met one of his parishioners. He told us that Van Truong was considered delusional because of his faith and committed to an asylum.'

'He has been released now.'

'But on condition that he signs a document certifying his mental illness, making him subject to readmission to an asylum should he "relapse".'

'It was an exceptional case. I agree that a confrontational approach is not always the best solution. In the future much will depend on whether the Party continues to adopt an approach that seeks to punish protesters, or focuses on entitlements in order to diminish the grounds for protest.

'After the war,' Kai continued, 'it was clear that if we were to carry out Ho's Marxism-Leninism we would have to develop a political system very different from those of our Southeast Asian neighbours. We were drawn to Marxism-Leninism because of its social theories and its criticism of capitalist economics. It was irrelevant at the time that Ho's ideology created self-imposed political barriers with the West and set us apart from other communist countries. This ethnocentric focus on our own affairs was complicated by the lack of international experience of our leaders whose foreign travel was limited to official visits to other communist countries. Also our military victories over reputedly superior military forces such as France, the United States, and, in 1979, China, created a sense of superiority that a wider world view would not justify. Because we identified communism with the historical goals of Vietnamese nationalism, the Party was enshrined with an aura of unquestionable truth, even when its policies resulted in failure.

'It is not a state of affairs,' Kai continued, 'that can be easily democratised. Vietnam is ruled by the Party's absolute authority through a network of party cadres at every level of social activity. All Vietnamese are expected to be members of one or other of the organizations led by party cadres, and all managers and military officials are ultimately answerable to party representatives. Not everyone is happy with the measures we use to ensure consensus. Occasionally it leads to abuses and corruption.'

'We need to introduce changes that include a free market system in order to stimulate our ailing economy. At the same time we must avoid becoming captive to the direct control of capital and from the impersonal control of market imperatives which, as Marx reminds us, subordinates human needs to the requirements of accumulation and profit-maximization.'

In spite of the caveat, it was a small concession. Even so Vietnam would have to wait for another generation of leaders before a more accountable form of government replaced a dictatorship demanding compliance, economic and political, not on the basis of social consensus, but on the dictates of Party bosses.

'Can we talk about Aquino,' Angel said, changing the subject. Ever since his last meeting with Aquino Angel had been worried about Aquino's state of mind. Dangerous at any time, an unstable Aquino could easily become out of control. 'A civilized Vietnam has no need of state-sponsored assassination. Let Aquino return to the Philippines.'

'I am not holding him. He is free to leave.'

'He thinks you would notify the Philippine police.'

'Why?'

'Because of what he knows.'

'The information would only incriminate himself. It is of no concern to us.'

'If occasion arises, would you use such a service again?'

'Extreme measures are sometimes necessary. Osama bin Laden's death is a case in point. Next to the Americans, who use significant resources to devising unhappy ends for inconvenient foreign leaders, our political assassinations are few and far between. Targeted killing is not always the best solution. There is always the possibility that the assassination of one leader may result in the rise of another even less to one's liking, or to a state of chaos more dangerous than the problem the killing was meant to solve. Then there is the problem of what to do with those who carry out this clandestine work. If Aquino wants to leave Vietnam he may do so. We have no interest in him.'

31

Nan was driven to her office near the Buoi market every morning by her driver. Although she had delegated much of her husband's work, she continued to work alongside her managers and oversee the direction of the company. Angel had begun work on a business plan for a Security Service for both the private and commercial sector. It did not look promising. Most security firms in Vietnam offered round-the-clock monitoring of factories, hospitals, schools, banks, and supermarkets. The only areas not fully covered were security-related networks and software systems for financial institutions.

Angel was on the terrace reading a prospectus published by Long Hai Security when he caught a glimpse of light from the fire escape on the apartment building on the opposite side of the street. Light reflected off gun metal has a peculiar cast: it gleams rather than shines, like the colour of a goshawk's wings.

Instinctively Angel got to his fee and cassually walked into the house. Once inside he quickly climbed the stairs to the bedroom on the first floor. Careful not to be seen through the window he took out Tien's old Mk 2 Lee-Enfield from the back of Nan's clothes cupboard. He inserted a single bullet into the ten-round box magazine and unlocked the safety catch.

The French windows in the bed room opened onto a balcony enclosed by a balustrade of multiple cast stone balusters. It was not ideal cover, since it was possible for someone on the fire escape to see between the baluster shafts. Angel trusted that the man's attention would be fixed on the terrace, waiting for his return.

The fire escape was partly hidden by a waist high brick wall concealing anyone sitting or crouching on the steps. If Angel was the sniper's target, the assassin would position himself between the first and second floor landing, high enough to have an unobstructed view over the garden wall, but not so high that the angle of fire was too acute for a clean shot.

Angel edged forward towards the balustrade, crawling on his stomach, one hand holding the Lee-Enfield in front of him, and sighted his rifle at the point where he saw the reflection.

It had to be Aquino.

The moment Angel saw the big man's head rise above the parapet he pulled the trigger. Aquino's head was thrown back by the impact of the bullet, his body disappearing behind the wall. The sound of the shot still ringing in his ears, Angel put the rifle back into its leather scabbard and returned it to the cupboard.

Aquino's body was not found for several hours. Vietnam has a low murder rate, 3 per 100,000 people. Being a foreigner, Aquino's death was immediately be reported to Kai. Learning the whereabouts of the shooting, Kai would guess what had happened. There would be no news report, and no investigation. Aquino would be numbered among the many unexplained deaths from Vietnam's prisons and 're-education' camps

Angel had killed before, but the enemy had been unknown, nameless and faceless, without personality or identity. The anonymity sanctioned wartime killing. One did not take a human life, just a figure in the form of a person.

When Angel caught up with Kai several weeks later, neither

man mentioned Aquino. It was as if there had been nothing positive in his life worth remembering. And yet Angel could not dismiss Aquino's death as being of no consequence. Life was still a life, and in itself the highest value. Although man's moral and spiritual life is in this world is a baffled and thwarted enterprise, Angel hoped that whatever grace of character Aquino possessed would find its fulfilment beyond the grave.

32

The largest security firm in Vietnam is the Long Hai Company run by Major General Phan Van Xoan, formerly Ho Chi Minh's body guard and commander-in-chief of the Ministry of the Interior's internal security division. His association with Ho gave him enormous prestige and influence with the Politburo. Consequently Van Xoan has a monopoly providing security guard services to a range of industries, construction sites, retail establishments, and warehouses. Other agencies were left to pick up less lucrative contracts.

Angel was facing a problem felt by many retired SAS officers. Trained for combat, there were few civilian jobs that demanded a high degree of expertise with weapons and knowledge of counter-insurgency warfare techniques. As a result many found work as security guards on construction sites, or in warehouses and factories, work Angel was not interest in.

Three weeks after Aquino's death Kai asked Angel to meet him for lunch at the French grill in the Marriott Hotel. Kai had reserved a table in the hotel's extraordinary protruding upper deck with views over the city. It was the first time Angel had met Kai outside his office, a suggestion on Kai's part rarely offered to even his closest friends and associates.

Over lunch Kai asked Angel about his plans for the future.

'I've been thinking of starting a business.'

'What kind of business?'

'Security. '

Kai shook his head. 'Van Xoan has the security business sewn up. Of course you could work for him, but it would be a waste of your experience and time.'

'Actually, I have come to the same conclusion.'

'Have you read about the terrorist attacks in Paris and elsewhere?' Kai asked.

'Yes. It still amazes me that people can believe that killing yourself and others will earn God's blessing. They must be so brainwashed that they no longer question the reasonableness of their choices.'

'But there are others,' Kai said, 'militant Islamic group like ISIL for whom suicide bombers are not the main form of attack. These people are more numerous and far more dangerous. In their hands terrorism is a specialized form of guerrilla warfare. It is waged across the globe rather than within the borders of a country targeted for revolutionary change.'

'I know. I have come across them in Africa and the Middle East.'

'As you say, terrorism knows no boundaries. The Bali bombing, the Marriott Hotel explosion, the attack on the Australian Embassy in Djakarta, and the capture of Islamabad terrorists in Thailand and Cambodia has brought the reality of such threats closer to home.'

'To Vietnam?'

'Yes. A Boeing 727 was hijacked near Phan Rang Air Base not long ago. When the pilot refused the highjacker's demands he set off his grenades. The plane plunged to the ground killing all 75 people aboard. It was an isolated incident, but we are certainly not immune.'

Kai paused. 'We do not have a counter-terrorism unit in

Vietnam. I would like you to set up a tactical unit to handle such threats. Would you be interested?'

Angel was taken aback. 'You mean work for the CPV?'

'Yes, but more specifically, with me. The task force will be a branch of the Ministry of State Security.'

'The people you recruit will need specialized training,' Angel said. 'You are going to have to work closely with your old nemesis.'

'What do you mean?'

'You will need to engage with the Bureau of Counter Terrorism. CT is an American agency. The Bureau is to terrorism what Interpol is to crime. It develops strategies and approaches to counter terrorism in cooperation with other agencies.'

'I can see to that.'

'You will also have to join the Antiterrorism Assistance Program, another American run organization. It is the primary provider of antiterrorism training and equipment to agencies throughout the world. '

'Would this mean employing Americans?'

'As consultants, and as the occasion demands. In addition to keeping tabs on terrorist networks, AAP mobilizes international support to counter violent extremism. Vietnam is not the only country with disaffected ethnic, racial or religious minority groups. Effective intervention involves more than a raid on an arm's dump, and restrictive laws that criminalize those who have no means of redress.'

'Our conflict with the Montagnards has a long history. Unfortunately it is being encouraged by Special Forces veterans, evangelical organizations and right-wing groups. But we are making concessions.'

Angel was sceptical that this was the case. He had seen little evidence of improvements in the Degar's standard of living. Police were still making arbitrary arrests and local cadres were appropriating private property. Such practices would draw the minorities into the terrorist camp, rather than have they become active suppliers of intelligence about terrorist plans.

'Other major considerations?' Kai asked.

'You will have to set up a financial intelligence unit that can identify illicit financing and analyse suspicious transactions. This may require a revision of your banking rules and the engagement of compliance officers to detect and prevent illicit money transfers. In spite of the likelihood of complaints from the international press you must be prepared to take action free from bureaucratic and external influence.' Angel paused. 'This is what countering a dirty war is really about – making one's country a hard target. It must be so costly to attack that no radical is willing to face the consequences.'

'That will also not be a problem.'

'I thought not.'

'May I take it,' Kai asked, 'that you are able to liaise with the organizations you mentioned, and integrate their services into our own anti-terrorist unit?'

'Yes. But we are racing ahead. I have not agreed to anything yet.'

'Understood. Unfortunately our constitution does not provide for foreigners to hold key government positions. But if you agree, I will see that you get a permanent residence card and all the entitlements accorded to the head of a ministerial-level agency.'

33

As Angel expected, Nan was not in favour of him working with Kai.

'I'm not a great fan of the Communist Party,' Angel said, 'but on the other hand the country needs an anti-terrorist organization. There are 72,000 Muslims in Vietnam, with 5,000 believers living in Ho Chi Minh City alone. Sooner or later someone will get radicalised and start setting off bombs.'

'There have been no terrorists related deaths in Vietnam.'

'No, but with 32,000 deaths last year from terrorist attacks, no country, not even Vietnam, can afford to ignore the threat. ISIL, al-Qaeda, Boko Haram, Al-Nusra and Jemaah Islamiyah operate across borders. No country is safe.'

'Why you, and why now?'

Aquino, Angel remembered, had asked the same question. 'I know more about countering terrorists than anyone on Kai's staff. I've spent most of my working life organizing and training anti-terrorist units and detecting and preventing terrorist threats. As for 'why now', the reason is clear enough. Terrorists have been active close to Vietnam: in Indonesia, Myanmar, Thailand, and the Philippines.'

'More fighting, more killing. Is it really necessary?'

'Terrorists have to be stopped. I don't know what motivates them. They claim it is religion. If so it is a religion that uses God in the service of other self-seeking motives. More likely they are totally dissatisfied with their own lives and are looking for a reason to justify their existence.'

'By killing others?'

'It gets them noticed.'

'Will you be fighting?'

'No.'

'You told me that you had done with warfare and violence.'

'Violence is good or bad depending on the use or purpose it is put to. Not to use violence against those for whom any crime is an unprincipled impulse to violence is to forego goodness for the sake of evil. Unless survival is a sin, violence must be kept in service of order and justice and even of peace. My opposition to violence and war is as strong as ever. But evil must be seen for what it is. One cannot suspend judgment just because we would prefer things to be otherwise.'

Nan gave a resigned shrug.

Although Angel told Kai he needed a couple of days to make up his mind, he knew that he would accept Kai's offer. Kai did not have to invent the threat of local terrorism. ISIL suicide bombers had recently launched a gun and bomb assault in Jakarta killing seven people. Working alongside Kai, Angel could take the defensive measures necessary to prevent such attacks from occurring locally. The unit would have a purely offensive mission, meeting evil with whatever force was necessary. There was no non-violent way of disarming those intent on murder.

34

Notwithstanding Ho Chi Minh's Proclamation of Independence, which took its cue from the American Declaration of Independence, the spoken and written word is monitored more aggressively in Vietnam than in any other country in Southeast Asia.

Kai excused this excess on the exclusive power of the leadership and their desire to maintain the constancy of the communist State. To this end Ho's prejudices against liberal democracy were transferred into law and became government policy affecting all areas of civil administration.

Angel knew there were a growing number of junior ministers who had not been selectively recruited and trained in political matters who were willing to move with the times. They knew that Marxist socialism (which sought to abolish the State) has always created an even bigger and more intrusive government than existed before and that economic activity isn't sustainable without pricing set by the free market.

Aware that Ho's ideology furnished the pretext for arbitrary laws, they were prepared to oppose the Party when these violated the Convention of Human Rights. Free thought, free belief, and freedom of expression – the most important things in a civilized country, fell under the hammer of communism under Ho's Leninist-Marxist policies. Given the institutionalized distrust of change it would take time to curb the tide of discriminatory measures and never-ending stream of directives which worked against individual freedom.

Although Kai had spoken of change, both the political system and the role of the Communist Party remain firmly intact. From the point of view of the Party, the legal system operates solely to support the state policy and policies of the Party. The Party's ability to influence institutions, including the courts, at all levels lies at the heart of its power. Without the behind the scenes influence over institutions, Party would immediately lose leverage and its preeminent place in the political system.

Managing the potential conflict between an increasingly independent judiciary and a political system that places a premium on control is a dynamic process. How the Party manage the growing contradiction between the development of a rule of law and the continued charismatic rule of the Party is a challenge. Nevertheless the Constitution is being reformed to redefine the status and role of the legislature, executive, and judiciary. Private ownership is now protected. The law is still discretionary, but public outcry has forced the government to reign in the power of the prosecutors and police and create accountability within the legal system.

35

The morning after their meeting at the Marriot, Angel received an urgent call from Kai asking him to his office.

Kai smiled on seeing Angel, but his manner was serious. 'We've had some troubling news. I told you that we had an agent among the Montagnards. He has learned that Ha Tay is sending a couple of his hit men to Hanoi. He wants you out of the way.'

'Ha Tay?'

'Tay is the gang boss that organized the attack on Mrs. Tien's warehouse. He also provided Moi with the manpower to break-in to our warehouse. These operations proved costly. Fifteen of his men were either killed or taken into custody. He blames you for this.'

'How would he know I had anything to do with these jobs?'

'Moi might have mentioned your name. We know Moi was behind the raid on our warehouse, and it is a fair guess that he was also behind the blackmail attempt on Mrs. Tien. I can't touch Tay unless I have more evidence. It might be just a rumour. In the mean time we will carry out checks on anyone coming into Hanoi from Son La where Tay hangs out.'

'Would Tay risk killing a foreigner?'

'It is unlikely. But he has suffered a huge loss of face. It is more common for the foreigner to be the guilty party. Monsignor Peter Dao Duc Diem was stabbed to death two weeks ago in Hue by a British citizen. Nationality is incidental if the motive is strong enough. I have put a car and driver at your disposal. The driver is armed. I have also ordered my men to keep watch on your house.'

Kai pulled out a drawer and passed Angel a long barrel .367 Magnum revolver in a shoulder holster and a box of flat-nosed bullets.

'You may like to have this,' Kai said, pushing the revolver across the table towards Angel.

'No. There is no need. Your men will be enough.'

Kai nodded. 'As I said it might be just a rumour. But in case it's not, we'll arrest any of Tay's men that put foot in Hanoi. We know who most of them are, and there is only one road into Hanoi from Son La.'

Outside Security Headquarters was a waiting unmarked black Vauxhall police car and a driver in plain clothes. On the passenger seat beside the driver was an H&K Semi-automatic Pistol.

It was war again.

A sigh of indescribable weariness passed from Angel's lips.

36

Angel not to tell Nan about Tay's threat, believing that it would only confirm in her mind the risks of working with Kai.

Check points and armed guards could prove only limited security. If Angel had relied on such measures when with the SAS he would not be alive today. Attack and defence are like two sides of a coin. Each side has advantages and disadvantages. Like many questions examining two possible solutions, it is the specific situation that determines the ultimate choice. While impatience can come with a cost, Angel decided to act first. It gave him the initiative, and if successful, would prevent any bloodshed.

Angel called Kai and outlined his idea. 'Success depends on whether you are prepared to make an enemy of Moi.'

'You mean because of his connections?'

'Yes.'

'Nepotism within the Party goes only so far.'

'Good. Then ask Moi to come your office tomorrow morning.'

Angel arrived at Security Headquarters shortly before Moi. When Moi was shown into Kai's office neither Kai nor Angel got to their feet. It was not the welcome Moi expected. Nor had he anticipated Angel's presence. Regaining his composure, Moi greeted Kai in Vietnamese.

Speaking deliberately in English, Kai asked Moi to be

seated. The turning towards Angel, Kia said, 'You know my colleague, Mr Angel?'

'Yes, we've met.' Moi nodded at Angel, surprised by Kai's use of the word 'colleague'. It suggested a close working relationship, not something that Moi had foreseen.

'Mr. Moi,' Kai continued, 'we know you were behind the arson attack on Mrs. Tien's warehouse.'

Moi opened his mouth to speak, but Kai waved him to silence. 'The evidence maybe circumstantial, but Tay will oblige us with a confession if we need it. But let us move on. Your plan to break into our warehouse was facilitated by the information we passed you. Even so it was a mistake to use your own transport. The registration numbers of all vehicles entering and leaving the port are recorded, and their times of arrival and departure noted.'

Moi's composure became less certain.

'Then again you should not have relied on Tay's men to carry out your plans. His men are petty crooks. They left a trail of clues: fingerprints, tools, and a drawing of the logo, the drawing given to you by Mr. Angel to identify the crates.'

Moi, his confidence shaken, seemed to shrink into himself. Stealing government property carried the death sentence.

Kai let Moi consider the implication of his words. It was possibly the worst few minutes of Moi's life.

Then it was Angel's turn to speak.

'Mr. Moi, Tay has decided to avenge his losses. He intends to have me killed. Whether he learned my role in your plans by chance or you mentioned my name is unimportant. It is important is that he drops this threat before more people get killed.'

Up to this point Angel had spoken in a quiet, almost

~ 164 ~

confidential matter of fact voice. But then his voice hardened, and moving closer to Moi, so that Moi felt the full weight of Angel's formidable presence, he said, 'Mr Moi, you will tell Tay that unless he drops this madcap idea I will take a team of commandos to Lao Cai. You will tell Tay that I will find him, and that I will kill him, and any of his men foolish enough to be with him. Do you understand what I am saying, Mr. Moi?'

Moi nodded. He understood very well.

'You have 24 hours to get back to Mr. Kai with Tay's answer. Do I make myself clear?'

Moi nodded again.

Kai's dismissal was curt. 'That is all for now Mr. Moi. You may go now.'

Moi got up. Like a schoolboy caught cheating he gave an anxious smile to both men before leaving.

Kai did not have to wait 24 hours for Moi's answer. Moi called back within the hour saying that Tay's vendetta against Angel was a rumour. Tay held no grudge against the Security Branch or Angel, that he was a loyal party member and could be relied upon to support the Minister in any way possible.

The contrition in Moi's voice accepted that no presidential intercession would save him if Kai decided to act. Neither Kai nor Angel were to cross paths with Moi again.

37

On his way home Angel bought a bunch of yellow Chrysanthemums, Nan's favourite flower. The Vietnamese believe that the orderly unfolding of the chrysanthemum's petals represent perfection. A petal of the flower placed at the bottom of a glass is believed to encourage a long and healthy life. That evening Nan found a yellow chrysanthemum petal in her wine glass.

Angel had seen the dark side of Vietnam, the ill-treatment of the minorities, violence against prisoners, corruption, an inept judiciary and secret police. But there were signs that the political situation was changing.

Eventually the doctrinaire policies of a miss-guided body of men would become antiquated, and the assumptions of those in power would be regarded as the obstinacy of an old guard that would not learn.

In spite of all the vicissitudes, Vietnam had become Angel's home. Kealy was right. Given time he would grow into the country, as the country would grow into him. Vietnam had become part of his internal landscape.

And then there was Nan.

Nan, who had given a new meaning to his life, and ended Angel's search for happiness. Their coming together was the result of circumstances that neither could have foreseen. Aquinas said that fate was the action of God's providence, and so it seemed to Angel. A late fragment of verse by Raymond Carver came to mind:

And did you get what
You wanted from this life, even so?
I did.
And what did you want
To call myself beloved, to feel myself
Beloved on the earth